A COMMUNICATIVE
APPROACH TO ENGLISH

交際英語

朱正 主編

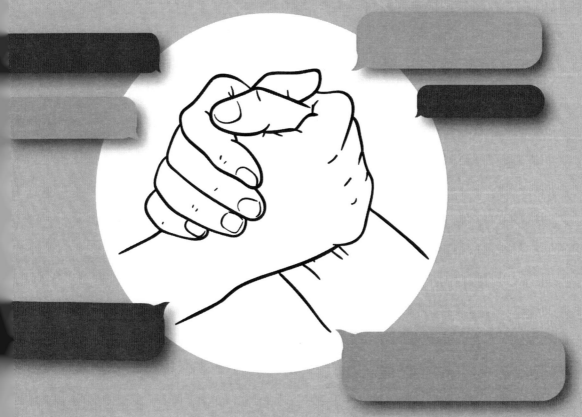

崧燁文化

目錄

前言

　　大學英語教學要重視培養學生運用語言進行交際的能力。在教學過程中教師既要傳授必要的語言知識，也要引導學生運用所學的語言知識和技能進行廣泛的語言交際活動。教學活動不但要有利於語言能力的訓練，也要有利於交際能力的培養。大綱的這一要求向傳統的語言教學提出了更高的要求：語言教學不僅要幫學生「輸入」語言，更重要的是如何引導學生「輸出」語言——這也正是交際教學法的關鍵，即：抓輸入方法和刺激活化學生的思考，刺激輸出的產生。

　　語言大師呂淑湘先生說：「語言的使用是一種技能，一種習慣。不同的語言當然要求不同的習慣，學習英語就是養成使用英語的習慣。一種習慣，只有透過正確地模仿和反覆地實踐才能養成。」也就是說，要學會英語，應該從模仿入手，經過反反覆覆的練習、應用，最終達到習慣成自然的境界。

　　為達到上述目的，本書的內容全部取材於日常生活、工作和一些熱門話題，具有涉及面廣、內容新穎、有啟示意義以及篇章短小、單字量小等特點。而且，本書中的語言點復現率比較高，這就更加便於學生模仿和記憶。此外，本書的五種練習項目均以提高英語聽說寫譯能力為目標，每一項都要求學生透過動口、動筆、動腦，並在課外查找和閱讀相關資料來完成。

　　使用本書的關鍵在於以學生為主、精講多練。在課堂上教師應以課文內容為基礎儘量創造機會讓學生練習聽說，使學生在練習和實踐中掌握課文。為了培養學生的自學能力，應督促學生充分做好預習和複習工作，因為只有預習和複習做到位了，學習效率才能提高，也才能使每一課的學習達到最佳效果。

　　本書可分六步進行：第一，課前師生討論課文內容。在上新課前教師可以提問一些與課文相關的思考題，目的是培養學生預習及閱讀時思考的習慣。討論形式可以多樣化。第二，教師對課文中的語言點進行講解。講解重點應放在詞語用法及使用場合上。為幫助學生正確掌握課文中的習慣用語，對比中英文語言及文化差異是非常必要的。第三，內容理解和討論。結合練習Ⅰ中和練習Ⅲ中的理解問答及討論題，聯繫現實生活，對每課的話題進行深入討論。第四，寫摘要。根據練習 II 的要求，指導學生把練習 I 中問題的答案用適當的連接詞連貫成一篇摘要，這樣做可以幫助學生逐漸擺脫想好中文再譯成英文的不良習慣。第五，漢譯英練習。以這樣六步處理課堂教學，既能使學生扎實地掌握所學內容，又有利於練好「聽說寫」基本功。

鑒於本書實用性強，也可供希望提高英語交際能力的社會人員自學使用。

由於編者程度有限，書中若有不周之處，請各位同仁提出寶貴意見，以便改進。

朱正

Book One

Lesson 1 A University Town

When we say that Cambridge is a university town we do not mean that it is a town with a university in it. A university town is one where there is no clear separation between the university building and the rest of the city. The university is not j ust one part of the town; it is all over the town. The heart of Cambridge has its shops, restaurants, market places and so on, but most of it is the college libraries, clubs and other places for university staff and students.

The town was there first. Cambridge became a center of learning in the thirteenth century. Many students were too poor to afford lodgings. Colleges were opened so that students could live cheaply. This was the beginning of the present-day college system.

Today there are nearly thirty colleges. Very few students can now live in college for the whole of their course; the numbers are too great. Many of them live in lodgings at first and move into college for their final year. But every student is a member of his college from the beginning. He must eat a number of meals in the college hall each week.

Students are not allowed to keep cars in Cambridge, so nearly all of them use bicycles. Don't try to drive through Cambridge during the five minutes between lectures, as you will find crowds of people on bicycles hurrying in all directions. If you are in Cambridge at five minutes to the hour any morning of the term, you'll know that you are in a university town. Stop in some safe place, and wait.

(273 words)

 Vocabulary

1. Cambridge   n. 劍橋（英國城市，劍橋大學所在地）

2. separation　　　n. 分離，分開

3. staff　　　　　　n. 全體職員

4. lodging　　　　　n. 寄宿處，寄宿

5. system　　　　　n. 系統，體系，制度，體制

 Useful Phrases and Expressions

1. When we say... we do not mean that...

2. The university is not j ust one part of the town; it is all over the town.

3. There is no clear separation between...

4. the present-day college

5. final year

6. Nearly all of them use...

7. You will find crowds of people on bicycles hurrying in all d-i rections.

 Exercises

Ⅰ.Comprehension Questions

1. What do people say about Cambridge?

2. Why is it a university town?

3. When was Cambridge University founded?

4. How many colleges are there in it now?

5. Where do the students live?

6. What does a student have to do once he has become a member of his college?

7. How do students move around the town?

8. Do students have cars? Why?

II .Essay Writing

Write an essay by putting together the answers to the questions in Exercise I, using such joining words as because, and, but and so on.

III .Questions for Discussion

1. Do you find it strange not to let the students keep cars in Cambridge? Why?

2. Use the library or Internet to find out how students learn in Cambridge. Give your comment on the way the students learn in that university.

3. Are there university towns in China? Do you think it is a good idea to have a university town? Why?

IV .Translation

Put the following Chinese into English, using as many as possible the phrases and expressions you have learned.

1. 在台灣不允許私人擁有槍枝。

2. 台灣是一個多方言國家。有的方言之間的差別很大，有的幾乎沒有什麼差別。

3. 我的班上不只我沒完成作業，還有好多學生也沒完成作業。

4. 今年是我姐姐大學最後一年，由於現在好工作不好找，現在她就開始到處找工作了。

5. 週末騎自行車遊台北城是個很有益的活動。

6. 一個班級如同一個家，每個學生都是這家庭中的一個成員，因此大家要愛護它。

7. 如今的茶館和 50 年前的不一樣。

Lesson 2　A Lucky Customer

All the housewives who went to the new supermarket had one great ambition: to be the lucky customer who did not have to pay for her shopping. For this was what the notice j ust inside the entrance promised. It said: "Remember, once a week, one of our customers gets free goods. This May Be Your Lucky Day!"

For several weeks Mrs.Edwards hoped, like many of her friends, to be the lucky customer. Unlike her friends, she never gave up hope. The cupboards in her kitchen were full of things which she did not need. Her husband tried to advise her against buying things but failed. She dreamed of the day when the manager of the supermarket would approach her and say: "Madam, this is Your Lucky Day. Everything in your basket is free."

One Friday morning, after she had finished her shopping and had taken it to her car, she found that she had forgotten to buy any tea. She dashed back to the supermarket, got the tea and went towards the cash-desk. As she did so, she saw the manager of the supermarket approach her. "Madam," he said, holding out his hand, "I want to congratulate you! You are our lucky customer and everything you have in your basket is free!"

(217 words)

 Vocabulary

1. supermarket　　n. 超級市場

2. ambition　　　n. 野心，雄心

3. entrance　　　n. 入口，門口，進入

4. cupboard　　　n. 餐櫃，櫥櫃

5. approach   n. 接近；方法，途徑／v. 接近，靠近

6. dash   vi. 快跑，猛擲，衝撞

7. cash   n. 現金

8. congratulate   vt. 祝賀，慶賀，恭喜

 ## Useful Phrases and Expressions

1. have one/a great ambition to be/that...

2. pay for one's shopping

3. This was what the notice promised.

4. get free goods

5. unlike...she never gave up hope

6. The cupboards in her kitchen were full of things which she did not need.

7. She dreamed of the day when...

8. The supermarket manager approached her.

9. Everything in your basket is free.

10. She finished her shopping.

11. dashed back to the supermarket

 ## Exercises

Ⅰ.Comprehension Questions

1. What was all the housewives' great ambition?

2. Where did the housewives do their shopping?

3. What attracted the housewives?

4. Did many of Mrs.Edwards' friends become the Lucky Customers?

5. What did they do?

6. Did Mrs.Edwards have any luck at first?

7. Did she give up?

8. What was her husband's idea to be the lucky customer?

9. Why did her husband want her to give up?

10. What happened to Mrs.Edwards on one Friday morning?

II .Essay Writing

Write an essay by putting together the answers to the questions in Exercise I, using such joining words as because, and, but and so on.

III .Questions for Discussion

1. Do you think the manager of the new supermarket was smart? Why?

2. What do you think of Mrs.Edwards?

3. If you were the manager, how would you attract more customers?

IV .Translation

Put the following Chinese into English, using as many as possible the phrases and expressions you have learned.

1. 我的一個好朋友有一個願望，希望他在 35 歲時能開一個大型的超市。

2. 很多中小學為他們的教師提供免費早餐和午餐。

3. 老馬今年 86 歲了，同其他老人不同的是，他特別喜歡旅遊，一年中的人有六個月都不在家。他的老伴特別為他擔心，建議他放棄這種愛好，因為像他這樣年紀的人在外面旅遊是很不安全的。

4. 現在有一種十元商店，店中的每樣商品都是十元，這種商店很受學生們的歡迎。

5. 我爺爺從不浪費，從不亂扔東西。這既是個好習慣，也是個壞習慣。如果你到他的屋子看看，你會立即發現那裡到處是無用的東西。

6. 一天下午，我買完東西走出超市時，看見一個小女孩向我走來。她站在我面前問我能否幫她。她說她的錢包被偷走了，沒錢回天津。那女孩看起來不像是騙人的，我就給了她 50 元。走時她記下了我的地址。一週後，我就收到了她寄回的 50 元。

Lesson 3   Save the Library

One of New York's most beautiful and valuable buildings is in danger. The New York Public Library, in the heart of the city at 42nd Street and Fifth Avenue, may have to close its doors.

The library is a very special place. Even though it is in the busiest part of the city, it has grass and trees around it, and benches for people to sit on. Even more unusual in crowded New York, its rooms are very large. The roof of the main reading room is fifty-one feet high. Here, a reader can sit and think and work in comfort.

And what books there are to work with! The library has over thirty million books and paintings. It owns one of the first copies of a Shakespeare play, a Bible printed by Gutenberg in the 15thcentury, and a letter written by Columbus in which he tells of finding the new world.

Every New Yorker can see and use the library's riches free.

But the cost of running the library has risen rapidly in recent years, and the library does not have enough money to continue its work. In the past, it was open every evening, and also on Saturdays and Sundays. Now it is closed at those times to save money.

The library is trying every possible way to raise more money to meet its increasing costs. Well-known New York writers and artists are trying to help. So are the universities, whose students use the library, and the governments of New York City and New York State. But the problem remains serious.

Yet a way must be found to save the library because, as one writer said, "The Public Library is the most important building in New York City—it contains all our knowledge."

(300 words)

 Vocabulary

1.	avenue	n. 林蔭道，大街，路
2.	unusual	adj. 與眾不同的，不尋常的
3.	Shakespeare	n. 莎士比亞
4.	bible	n. 《聖經》
5.	riches [複]	n. 財富，財產
6.	New York	n. 紐約
7.	remain	vi. 保持，逗留，剩餘，殘存

 Useful Phrases and Expressions

1. One of New York's most beautiful and valuable buildings is in danger.

2. in the heart of the city

3. may have to close its doors

4. A reader can sit and think and work in comfort.

5. And what books there are to work with!

6. He tells of finding the new word.

7. use the library free

8. The cost of running the library has risen rapidly.

9. The library is trying in every possible way to raise money to meet its increasing costs.

10. The problem remains serious.

11. A way must be found to save the library.

 **Exercises**

I .Comprehension Questions

1. What part of New York City is the Public Library in?

2. Why is it so famous?

3. What is so special about this library?

4. What about its opening hours?

5. Does the library run into trouble? What is the trouble?

6. Are there any people who are helpful in helping the library get out of difficulties?

7. What is the result?

8. What should be done then?

II .Essay Writing

Write an essay by putting together the answers to the questions in Exercise I, using such joining words as because, and, but and so on.

III .Questions for Discussion

1. Talk about a library you know.

2. Do you think we should have more public libraries in cities? Why?

IV .Translation

Put the following Chinese into English, using as many as possible the phrases and expressions you have learned.

1. 現在有些家長想盡一切辦法要把自己的孩子送到國外念書。出國念書是件好事，但是有些孩子高中還沒有讀就出國念書，效果會好嗎？

2. 有些中學不斷有學生輟學的原因是上學的費用不斷上漲。

3. 「SARS」期間，有些城市的公園免費為百姓開放，而且開放時間從 12 小時延長到了 16 小時，這種做法深受百姓歡迎。

4. 美國目前正在建築一條長達 4180 公里的「綠色走廊（Green Corridor）」。它是一條專為人們遠足、騎車旅遊的公路，汽機車不能使用。這條公路沿著東部沿海的緬因州（Maine）延伸到佛羅里達州的邁阿密（Miami）。

5. 學院學習環境要比前幾年好多了，新的教學大樓裡有很多寬敞的教室。晚上和週末，學生可以在舒適的環境中學習和思考問題。

Lesson 4   A Market Place for Toronto

Rienzi Salvatori is determined that the city of Toronto will have an outdoor marketplace for merchants from its immigrant community, complete with dancing and other forms of amusement from their native countries. "Toronto is truly multicultural," he said in a newspaper interview. "It's a city from many places, and a multicultural marketplace will help Torontonians to understand and appreciate the rich variety of cultural groups in our city."

Salvatori, aged 23, will soon complete his studies at the University of Toronto. He was eleven years old when he came to Canada from Italy with his parents. "Most of Toronto's immigrants are from lands where the marketplace has always been part of daily life," he said.

Salvatori has been interested in getting an open-air market for Toronto for the last three years. This year, with the help of two fellow students, he prepared a proposal on the subj ect and presented it to the city's Executive Committee, asking for their support. The proposal pointed out Toronto's rich variety of national groups, "whose customs include market shopping."

Under a Canadian government program for multiculturalism, the three students have received two thousand dollars with which they will do a study to find out whether Toronto's immigrant businessmen would support an open-air market. They hope the merchants will support the plan strongly. "A study done earlier this year showed that 90 percent of shoppers would be in favor of it," Salvatori said. "At first it would be an experiment. But we think it will prove to be good business for the merchants, as well as a tourist attraction."

(261 words)

Vocabulary

1. outdoor	adj. 室外的，戶外的，野外的
2. marketplace	n. 集會場所，市場，商場
3. merchant	n. 商人，批發商，貿易商
4. immigrant	adj.（外國）移來的，移民的／n. 移民
5. community	n. 公社，團體，社會
6. amusement	n. 娛樂，消遣，娛樂活動
7. multicultural	adj. 多元文化的
8. appreciate	vt. 賞識，鑑賞，感激
9. cultural	adj. 文化的
10. aged	adj. 老的，舊的，年老的
11. Italy	n. 義大利（歐洲南部國家）
12. proposal	n. 提議，建議
13. executive	adj. 實行的，執行的，行政的
14. committee	n. 委員會
15. multiculturalism	n. 多元文化性
16. strongly	adv. 強有力地，堅固地，激烈地

Useful Phrases and Expressions

1. He is determined that the city of Toronto will have an outdoor marketplace.

2. immigrant community

3. native countries

4. Toronto is truly multicultural.

5. the rich variety of cultural groups in our city

6. complete his studies at the University of...

7. The marketplace has always been part of daily life.

8. an open-air market

9. With the help of two fellow students, he prepared a proposal on...

10. They hope the merchants will support the plan strongly.

11. be in favor of it

 Exercises

I .Comprehension Questions

1. Who is Rienzi Salvatori?

2. What is his ambition?

3. Why does he want Toronto to have an outdoor market?

4. Why does he want to have dancing and other forms of amusement at the market?

5. Is he himself going to build the open-air market? How is he going to realize his plan?

6. What does the Canadian government want Salvatori and his fellow students to do?

7. What does their study show?

8. Is it likely that Toronto will soon have an open-air market? Why?

II .Essay Writing

   Write an essay by putting together the answers to the questions in Exercise I, using such joining words as because, and, but and so on.

III .Questions for Discussion

1. Do you think open-air markets in many ways are better than supermarkets? What are your reasons?

2. Many Chinese people like to do shopping in the open-air markets or farmers' markets. Why? What role do the open-air markets play in people's everyday life?

IV .Translation

Put the following Chinese into English, using as many as possible the phrases and expressions you have learned.

李強今年 50 歲，蘇州人。20 年前他獨自去美國華盛頓謀生，希望能生活得更好些。去美國之前，他是蘇州一家有名餐館的大廚。剛到華盛頓時，他在一家中國餐館當廚師。這家中國餐館很有名，美國總統和政府的官員都曾去過那裡用餐。在到美國的第八個年頭他離開了這家餐館，自己開了一家麵館。在開麵館之前他做了一下市場調查，發現中國麵條在當地很有市場。在華盛頓有不少華人都愛吃本土的麵條，而且，很多美國人對中國麵條也比較青睞。他把這些想法告訴了他在美國的姨媽，她非常支持他的想法。就這樣，李強麵館就開張了。當時華盛頓沒有幾家道地的中國麵館，所以他的生意特別好。現在華盛頓附近幾個城市裡都有他的分店。李強麵館以其豐富的品種、道地的口味吸引了很多的顧客。

Lesson 5   The Cost of Food

It is true it costs a lot to feed your family but you spend a much smaller part of your money on food than you did some years ago. In the United States people spend on food only about one dollar out of every five they earn. This is a smaller part than families spend today in other countries. In Europe, for example, a family spends a little more than half of its money on food.

Your money goes first on food. You spend the part that is left on your home, clothes and other things. If it is a large part, you are well off. Any country whose people spend the smaller part of their earnings on food has a high standard of living. But in every country, prices and costs change all the time. Have you heard about the "good old days" in the United States when beef was 15 cents a pound and bread was two loaves for five cents? You may wish prices were like that today. But in 1920, the average American family earned only $11 a week and spent almost 5 of that on food.

What counts is how much work we must do to pay for what we buy. For an hour's work, in 1931 an American factory worker could buy less than a pound and half of beef. Today he can buy more than three pounds. The price of beef is higher now, but the worker buys it with a smaller part of what he earns. He has more money left for other things. His standard of living is higher than before.

The food in stores is cleaner and better today, too. In the old days food was kept in open boxes and tubs. Today it is packed and displayed in cleaner ways. People can buy more kinds of food than ever before. 80 years ago, most stores had about 100 kinds of food, but now most medium-sized food stores sell about 8000 and they sell fresh foods all year round. Many prepared foods are almost ready for busy mothers to put on the table. Babies can have more good foods and grow better. Today children are taller and heavier.

In some countries, a farmer still grows only enough food for four or five people. In the United States a farmer grows enough for more than 50 people. New machines, new feeds for animals, better seeds, new ways of farming and shipping all have made it possible for farmers to produce more and better foods and put them in our stores.

It has taken us many years to learn how to provide these foods. But now we are sure that people all over the world can someday have a high standard of living.

(463 words)

 Vocabulary

1. earnings [複]　n. 所得，收入

2. loaf　　　　　n. 一條麵包，塊，遊蕩

3. tub　　　　　n. 桶，器皿，容器

4. display　　　vt. 陳列，展覽，顯示

5. medium　　　adj. 中間的，中等的

 Useful Phrases and Expressions

1. It is true that...

2. It costs a lot to feed a family.

3. Your money goes first for food.

4. spend one dollar out of every five they earn (for food)

5. You spend the part that is left on your home, clothes and other things.

6. A country whose people spend the smaller part of their earnings has a high standard of living.

7. good old days

8. Bread was two loaves for five cents.

9. average American families

10. What counts is how much work we must do to pay for what we buy.

11. The worker buys it with a smaller part of what he earns.

12. He has more money left for other things.

13. in the old days

14. all year around

15. Many prepared foods are ready for busy mothers to put on the table.

16. Babies grow better, and children are taller and heavier.

17. A farmer grows enough food for...

18. New machines, new feeds for animals... have made it possible for farmers to...

19. new way of farming

20. It has taken us many years to learn...

21. You are well off.

 Exercises

I .Comprehension Questions

1. Where does your money go first?

2. What do you do with the part of money that is left?

3. How can you tell you are well off?

4. How do we know a country whose people have a high standard of living?

5. But prices and costs change all the time in every country. Is there another way to tell people's living standard?

6. Why is the food in stores cleaner and better today?

7. How many kinds of foods did most stores have in the old days?

8. How many kinds of foods do most medium-sized food stores sell?

9. Do they sell fresh food all the year round?

10. Are there many prepared foods available for busy mothers to put on the table?

11. How come that babies grow better and children are taller and heavier today?

12. What have made it possible for farmers to produce more and better foods for people?

13. What conclusion can you draw from the above facts?

II .Essay Writing

Write an essay by putting together the answers to the questions in Exercise I, using such joining words as because, and, but and so on.

III .Questions for Discussion

1. Is the living standard of your family higher than 15 years ago? What are your reasons?

2. How can we help farmers in our country to improve their standard of living?

IV .Translation

Put the following Chinese into English, using as many as possible the phrases and expressions you have learned.

自從 1980 年以來，中國人民的生活水準確實有了很大的提高。人們買大而漂亮的房子、汽車和高檔的衣服，還經常到高級飯店用餐，到全國各地旅遊。去新、馬、泰、日本、澳洲等國旅遊的人越來越多。去美國、歐洲各國旅遊的人數每年都在增長。人們把自己的孩子送到國外去念書已不是新聞。所有這一切都表明人們支付飲食費用後還剩餘很多錢。

然而，並不是每個中國人都這樣富裕。他們中不少人賺的工資首先是滿足吃飯，吃飯的錢占去了他們工資的 80% 或更多，這樣剩下用於其他方面的錢就很少了。他們中有些人甚至沒錢讓孩子上學。還要經過數年，中國才能真正達到共同富裕，過上小康生活。

Lesson 6　Population

For many years, the world has been growing rapidly. In 1981, the world population was about four billion, four hundred and ninety million and in 2001, it was six and a half billion. If the population continues to increase at the same rate, the population of the world will be about 9 billion by 2050. In the last 30 seconds about 115 babies were born. During the same 30 seconds about 45 people died. This means 140 people are added to the world population every minute.

Many scientists and economists believe that food production will not keep up with population growth. No one knows how many people the earth can support, but many people believe that the world will soon be overpopulated. If the population were distributed evenly throughout the world, there would be about thirty persons per square kilometer of land. However, people aren't distributed evenly. In some parts of the world, there are as many as four hundred persons per square kilometer. The highest population density is in Europe and Asia.

Many people believe that such a high population would cause famine, wars, and other disasters. However, other people feel that the world could support a much larger population if its resources, such as food, energy, and land, were distributed equally. They also think that increased food production and technological improvements will solve the problem.

Since 1960, there has been a great increase in food production. Unfortunately, the population in many developing countries has risen faster than the rate of food production. Africa and South America have an annual population growth of 2.8 percent. As a result more and more people from developing countries are emmigrating to some developed countries. And that will create new problems.

(288 words)

 Vocabulary

1. rapidly　adv. 迅速地

2. billion　n. & adj. 十億（的）

3. rate n. 比率，速度，等級

4. means　n. 手段，方法

5. economist n. 經濟學者，經濟學家

6. growth　n. 生長，種植，栽培，發育

7. overpopulated　adj. 人口過密的

8. distribute vt. 散布，分布

9. evenly　adv. 均勻地，平坦地

10. per prep. 每，每一，由，經

11. density　n. 密度

12. famine　n. 饑荒

13. disaster　n. 災難，天災，災禍

14. resource　n. 資源，財力，辦法

15. equally　adv. 相等地，平等地，公平地

16. technological　adj. 科技的

17. improvement　n. 改進，進步

18. solve　vt. 解決，解答

19. unfortunately　adv. 不幸地

20. annual   adj. 一年一次的，每年的

21. emmigrate   vt. 移居外國；移出

22. create   vt. 創造，創作，引起，造成

 Useful Phrases and Expressions

1. The world population has been growing rapidly.

2. If the population continues to increase at the same rate...

3. This means 140 people are added to the world population every minute.

4. Food production will not keep up with population growth.

5. No one knows how many people the earth can support.

6. The world will soon be overpopulated.

7. If the population were distributed evenly throughout the world...

8. highest population density

9. Increased food production and technological improvement will solve the problem.

10. There has been a great increase in food production.

11. The population has risen faster than the rate of food production.

     People are emmigrating to...

Exercises

Ⅰ. Comprehension Questions

1. Why is it said that for many years, the world population has been growing rapidly?

2. What do many scientists and economists think of this rapid growth of population?

3. Does everybody share their view?

4. What do other people think?

5. What is the population situation in many developing countries?

6. What is the result of a large number of people who emmigrate to developed countries?

II .Essay Writing

Write an essay by putting together the answers to the questions in Exercise I, using such joining words as because, and, but and so on.

III .Questions for Discussion

1. There are two different views on population. Which one are you for? What are your reasons?

2. Do you think China has too many people? Why? What size of population is suitable for China?

IV .Translation

Put the following Chinese into English, using as many as possible the phrases and expressions you have learned.

在北京，如果你上班地點離家不近，8：00 上班，不想遲到的話，你最好 6：45 就出門。如果你住得很遠，在城的另一邊，你必須再提前半小時出門。10 年前每天早晨的上班高峰是 7：30 開始，下午下班的高峰是 6：00 開始。可是現在早晨高峰 7：00 就開始，下午 4：30 開始，而且高峰時間越來越長。早晨兩個半小時，下午三個小時。城區有些地段，沒有高峰時段，整天都是高峰期。為什麼會這樣？道理很簡單，私家車和公共汽車的數量近 10 年內猛增。目前北京的機動車（motor vehicles）達 400 多萬輛。雖然市政府建造了不少新道路，但仍然不夠，道路的建設跟不上汽車增長的速度。現在北京的出租車就有 6.7 萬多輛，私家車已突破 156 萬輛。讓人擔心的是，要買車的人越來越多。因為汽車越來越便宜，很多人認為如果汽車按目前的速度增加，不出 20 年北京所有的道路上就會全擠滿了汽車，到那時走路比開車還要快。車多交通事故就多，譬如今年 6 月份，交通事故大增，幾乎每天都有人死於交通事故。

Lesson 7   The Neighborhood Luncheonette

Marty's Luncheonette, at 232 Sherman Avenue, near 207th Street in New York City, is long and narrow, with light brown walls and a white counter with fourteen seats. Marty Rubin and his wife, Esther, have owned Marty's for almost twenty-five years. Most of the customers live or work in the neighborhood and come to the restaurant because of Esther Rubin's good cooking.

Marty Rubin opens up the restaurant every morning at 7:30 A.M. He and Esther's sister, Gussie Markowitz, take care of the customers at breakfast. At 10:30 A.M. Marty leaves for his house in Yonkers to get Esther, who has spent the morning in her kitchen. One day not long ago, Marty and Esther returned to the restaurant at 11:40 A.M. with eight roasts, eight meat loaves, twenty pounds of potato salad, twenty pounds of cole slaw, and a chocolate cake. There were only four people at the counter. Five minutes later, all fourteen seats were filled. From 11:45 A.M. until 1:30 P.M., the counter was full and there were always two or three people standing and waiting for a seat to be empty.

During that hour and three quarters, Marty, Esther, and Gussie didn't stop moving. Marty was at the cash register and made cold drinks. Esther and Gussie served the hot food and the coffee and made sandwiches. The customers came in, ordered their food, waited quietly, ate quickly, paid, and left. The people were friendly and most of them seemed to know each other.

From about 1:45 P.M., when Marty's closes, there is not much business. Marty, Esther, and Gussie have their own lunches and prepare for the next day. One day a woman who used to live in the neighborhood before she moved to a house in New Jersey came in for a cup of coffee at two o'clock. "I wish I could move back here," she said. "Where I live now, everybody is so busy with his own house that he has no time to talk or be friendly. There's no place like Marty's. I miss it."

(343 words)

 Vocabulary

1. neighborhood	n. 附近，鄰近	
2. Sherman	謝爾曼（姓氏，男子名）	
3. counter	n. 櫃臺	
4. roast	n. 烤好的一大塊肉／v. 烘烤	
5. salad	n. 沙拉	
6. cole	n. 油菜，小菜	
7. slaw	n. 高麗菜沙拉	
8. register	n. 出納機，收銀機	
9. Gussie	n. 格西（Augusta 的暱稱）	
10. New Jersey	n. 紐澤西州	

 Useful Phrases and Expressions

1. The customers come to the restaurant because of Esther's good cooking.

2. Marty Rubin opens up the restaurant every morning at 7:30 A.M..

3. take care of the customers at breakfast

4. Esther has spent the morning in the kitchen.

5. All the seats are filled.

6. The counter was full.

7. There were always two or three people standing and waiting for a seat to be empty.

8. During that hour and three quarters, Marty, Esther didn't stop moving.

9. There is not much business.

10. There is no place like Marty's.

 Exercises

I .Comprehension Questions

1. Who are Marty Rubin and Esther?

2. What do they do for a living?

3. How big is their restaurant?

4. For how long have they had the restaurant?

5. Does the restaurant stay open all day?

6. Is their business good?

7. Who come to eat there?

8. Why do people like to eat there?

9. Apart from their good cooking ' what is the thing that attracts people?

10. Can you give a similar example?

II .Essay Writing

Write an essay by putting together the answers to the questions in Exercise I, using such joining words as because, and, but and so on.

III .Questions for Discussion

1.Why is Marty's Luncheonette so successful? Can you find anything like it in our country?

2.Where can you find real life of a big city? Why? In the city what are the things that attract people most? Why?

IV .Translation

Put the following Chinese into English, using as many as possible the phrases and expressions you have learned.

有家餐館知名度很高。餐館不大，只有五張桌子，但很乾淨，服務周到，菜的價格雖比一般小飯館貴，但飯菜質量好，味道好，因此去的人很多。有時候去晚了，連空位子都沒了。每天總有人在外面排隊等候用餐。

店主是一對中年夫婦，丈夫叫張國強，妻子叫王玉娟。他們的工廠關門，夫婦倆雙雙失業。由於王玉娟會做一手地道的泰國菜，因此他們決定開一家小餐館謀生。早上供應麵條和餛飩，中午供應午餐。每天早上 6：00 就開門營業，一直到下午 2：30。一開始營業他倆就忙個不停，但很開心。每天早上要賣近 300 碗麵條和餛飩。有的人住得很遠也趕來吃他倆做的麵條和餛飩。每天中午也總是客滿，有一半的客人是回頭客。如果你要去吃飯的話，最好預先訂位，不然就要等。

Lesson 8   Farming in the City

With improvements in health care over the years, more Americans are living longer. Most of these people retire when they are about sixty-five years old, and sometimes they have problems afterward because they do not have much to keep them busy and interested. Many people and organizations are trying to change this by helping senior citizens with their problems, seeing to it that they live comfortably and keep active.

But there are some old people who never want to retire, and who keep on doing the things they love and doing them very well indeed. John Hart is typical.

The drivers on Central Avenue, one of the busiest streets in Albany, New York, may not notice John Hart's farm. But John Hart is there, growing his vegetables, just as he has been since he was thirteen. That was in 1930, ten years after he and his family got there in a one-horse carriage. It was all farmland then.

Most of the original farm is gone, but enough remains to keep John Hart busy. He left school when he was very young, and has worked as a farmer ever since. His elder sister, Margaret, has been with him all this time, and still helps in the kitchen.

Hart has slowed down a little in the last few years, but he is still out every day, often working on his hands and knees, sometimes using machines. A year ago he became ill and spent some time in the hospital. When he left, the doctors warned him to take it easy. "But I went right back to work the same as always. And when the doctors examined me, they said, 'You're doing fine. Whatever you're doing, keep on doing it'."

Hart says he will never retire. "I couldn't sit around and do nothing. I'm better off if I keep moving," he says. And John Hart does keep moving and working, though he is slow and bent over with age.

But his mind is young. "If there's a way to do something better, of course I'd change," he says with a laugh. "I'll tell you one thing I learned. No matter how old you get, you can always learn something."

(373 words)

 ## Vocabulary

1.	retire	vi. 退休，引退，退卻
2.	afterward	adv. 然後，後來
3.	organization	n. 組織，機構，團體
4.	senior	adj. 年長的，資格較老的，高級的
5.	typical	adj. 典型的，象徵性的
6.	Albany	n. 奧爾巴尼（美國紐約州的首府）
7.	carriage	n. 馬車，客車
8.	farmland	n. 農田
9.	original	adj. 最初的，原始的
10.	bent	adj. 彎的，彎曲的

 ## Useful Phrases and Expressions

1. With improvement in health care, people are living longer.

2. They do not have much to keep them busy and interested.

3. See to it that they live comfortably and keep active.

4. notice sth.

5. Most of the original farm is gone.

6. His elder sister has been with him all the time and still helps in the kitchen.

7. Hart has slowed down a little.

8. work on one's hands and knees

9. warn him to take it easy

10. I went right back to work the same as always.

11. You're doing fine.

12. Whatever you're doing, keep on doing it.

13. I couldn't sit around and do nothing.

14. He is slow and bent over with age.

15. His mind is young.

 Exercises

I .Comprehension Questions

1. Why are nowadays people living longer?

2. What is the problem that old people usually have?

3. Do all the old people have this problem?

4. Where is Mr.Hart's farm?

5. How is it that his farm is in a busy street?

6. What does he do in his farm? How long has he been doing farm work?

7. What did the doctors advise him?

8. Did he take the doctors'advice?

9. What does he say to other people?

10. What does he believe in life?

II .Essay Writing

Write an essay by putting together the answers to the questions in Exercise I, using such joining words as because, and, but and so on.

III .Questions for Discussion

1. Can you understand that some old people never want to retire? Why?

2. What do you think is the best way to spend one's retirement? Why?

IV .Translation

Put the following Chinese into English, using as many as possible the phrases and expressions you have learned.

1. 隨著生活水準的提高，搭乘飛機旅遊的人越來越多。

2. 王越教授今年 102 歲了，如今生活還能自理。他的家裡全是書。他從來沒有感到無聊、無事可做。他每天看書看報。他的長壽祕訣是活到老學到老，常用腦，勤思考。

3. 這輛腳踏車看樣子很舊，但它很好騎，很輕。我已騎了 40 年了，從不出毛病。這輛車是考上大學後老爸作為禮物送給我的。

4. 由於要修高速公路，我的地被政府徵收了。這樣我就沒有田可種。我沒讀什麼書，除了會種田，其他什麼都不會做，整天在家裡沒事幹，生活一天比一天難過。父母說這樣下去不行，不如全家去郊區種蔬菜。就這樣我們到了郊外，租了塊地，開始種蔬菜。當然很辛苦，一年四季都有活。但一年下來我們可以賺到 30 萬元。今年冬天我們不那麼認真，休整了一下。明年春天我們準備一邊種菜一邊辦一個養豬場。如果做得好，一年下來可賺到 50 萬多元。

Lesson 9　Mr. and Mrs.Trucker

Rolling along the nation's highways, hundreds of wives of longdistance truck drivers are teaming up with their husbands these days. Like the Hodges, the couples share the driving, receive two salaries, and end the loneliness that is so much a part of the lives of most long-distance truckers and the women they leave behind.

No one knows exactly how many of these husband-and-wife teams there are, but at certain big truck stops, as many as eighty to a hundred of them are seen per week and the number is growing.

"We think it works out fine," says Richard Beauchamp, president of Refrigerated Transport, Inc., of Atlanta, Georgia, one of the first companies to accept the "mom-and-pop" idea. Seven years ago, he did not have any man-and-wife teams. Now he has fifty of them working on his company's 650 trucks. Mr.Beauchamp says he would like to have a wife in every cab.

"People say women can't drive trucks, but it isn't true," he says. "Most of our women drivers are just as good as men, and some are better. These new trucks j ust aren't that hard to drive."

"Most of our women drivers are between thirty-eight and fiftyeight years of age. Their children are grown up or in college, so they can get away from home easily," Mr.Beauchamp continues.

Mr. and Mrs.Hodge, who were married a year ago and have no children, described their new way of life, while refueling at a truck stop near Mesquite, Texas. Their truck was packed with more than thirty thousand pounds of refrigerated chicken parts, which they were taking from Alabama to California.

"I wouldn't team up with any man," Mr.Hodge said over a cup of coffee, while his wife fixed her hair in front of the huge side-view mirror of their truck. "Driving with another man is like being married to him. If you don't get along well, it can be terrible; you're locked up together in that cab, and you can really get to hate one another. Bringing Virginia along was the smartest thing I ever did. It's a wonderful life for a husband and wife."

His wife said, "Usually I drive for five hours and he drives for five. I stay mostly on the big highways because it's easier. He drives in the towns and does the parking and backing up."

Their air-conditioned truck has a bed behind the driver's seat where one can sleep while the other drives. Some trucks even have television sets that the off-duty driver can watch as the truck rolls along the road, but the Hodges'only entertainment is a radio.

The Hodges are pleased with their work. "The two of us make good money and enjoy good company," Mr.Hodge said.

"If I had known this, I might have married a truck driver a long time ago," his wife added.

(481 words)

 Vocabulary

1. loneliness	n. 孤獨，寂寞	
2. exactly	adv. 正確地，嚴密地	
3. refrigerate	vt. 使冷卻，使變冷，冷藏	
4. Georgia	n. 喬治亞州（在美國南部，首府在 Atlanta）	
5. refuel	v. 補給燃料	
6. Alabama	n. 阿拉巴馬州（美國的一個州）	

7. fix   vt. 安裝，準備，固定

8. mirror   n. 鏡子

9. view   n. 景色，風景

10. entertainment   n. 娛樂，娛樂表演

 Useful Phrases and Expressions

1. team up with

2. That is so much a part of the lives of...

3. at big truck stops

4. As many as eighty to a hundred of them are seen per week.

5. The number is growing.

6. It works out fine.

7. He has fifty of them working on his company's 650 trucks.

8. These new trucks just aren't hard to drive.

9. Their children are grown up or in college.

10. They can get away from home easily.

11. Their truck is/was packed with refrigerated chicken parts.

12. side-view mirror

13. be married to

14. Bringing Virginia along was the smartest thing I ever did.

15. off-duty driver

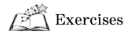 **Exercises**

I.Comprehension Questions

1. What can one often see on the American highways?

2. Is this idea of husband-and-wife team good?

3. What is so good about this idea?

4. How old are most of the women drivers?

5. Why are they able to get away from home?

6. Do the husband-and-wife teams enjoy this way of life? Is there anything to prove this? Give an example.

7. How do Mr. and Mrs.Hodge cooperate with each other?

8. What do the Hodges say about their work?

II.Essay Writing

Write an essay by putting together the answers to the questions in Exercise I, using such joining words as because, and, but and so on.

III.Questions for Discussion

1. In many jobs husbands and wives can work together. There are a lot of advantages of this idea. What do you think? Are there any disadvantages?

2. In future do you wish to work together with your spouse? Why?

IV.Translation

Put the following Chinese into English, using as many as possible the phrases and expressions you have learned.

1. 有人說豆腐是日本人發明的，這不是事實。豆腐是道道地地的中國食品。中國人已食用了兩千年。從前人們把豆腐稱為窮人吃的肉。到明代有錢人才開始吃豆腐。科學家一直在研究豆腐是何人在什麼時候發明的,可是至今沒有人真正知道。但許多考古學者(archaeologist)都認為豆腐起源於漢代。

2. 有一對退休夫婦,丈夫叫王天鵬,妻子叫張雅文。他們的孩子都長大了,一個在大學讀書,另一個已成家了。他們每天很空閒,沒有什麼事可做,常常感到寂寞,總想找點事情做做。有一天午飯後,妻子建議他們辦一個夫妻托兒所。他們住的地方周圍沒有托兒所,丈夫很同意這個想法。對他們來說,辦一個托兒所不是很困難,因為在退休前兩人都是小學教師。於是,他們把這想法告訴了管委會,管委會十分支持他們。就這樣,他們的托兒所辦起來了,一切都很順利。周圍的人紛紛把孩子送到他們的托兒所。大家都說他倆辦了件大好事。現在他們每天很忙,但很開心。

Lesson 10   Women's Liberation : a Long Way to Go

In the 1960s and 1970s attention began to be paid to women's liberation, and a serious attempt was made by women to get equal rights and treatment. The story has usually been the same. When a woman looks for work, the first question she is asked is, "Can you type?" No consideration is given to the woman's mind or schooling or qualifications. Women have been thought of only as office workers in government and business, but not as officers; as nurses and teachers, but not as doctors and lawyers. People had a picture in their minds of women happily working in their homes and not wanting to change. The result has been that in most cases they have not been allowed to change, even if they want to.

But slowly the prej udice against women is weakening and the idea of liberation is becoming stronger. Women are taking more and more important jobs in business, government, and the arts and many times are not waiting for men to lead. "Women's lib" has in fact become one of the most important movements in the United States and Canada, and, indeed, the world. Women get together in small groups for "consciousness-raising" meetings, to bring to one another their own experiences as second-class human beings, in their homes and marriages as well as at work and in school.

This has led to much discussion about marriage and family life, particularly in regard to what a woman's role and duties should be. The result has been that many more women are not only going to work but are having their own careers, their own friends, and their own interests, quite apart from those of their husbands. At the same time many husbands have accepted the fact that they themselves will have to play a different family role to help more with housework and with the children and to recognize their wives'rights and wishes. In short, women are no longer accepting their positions as "prisoners" in their homes, but are fighting to gain accep-tance for themselves as full and important human beings.

Without question, women's lives are improving. But still not all women support the women's liberation movement. Particularly in small towns, the idea is not taken seriously. Take, for example, the village of Hope, Indiana, with fifteen hundred people (and quite like many other small towns elsewhere). Mrs.Katherine Stafford says: "What you have here are a lot of happy women. Maybe if they weren't so happy, there might be more interest in women's liberation."

Mrs.Judy Douglas says: "I don't want equal rights with men; I believe the man should be the head of the house. I want to cook and clean and do the work women are supposed to do. How could any woman be happier than that?"

Change may come slowly to Hope, but those who believe in women's liberation continue to hope, and to work, for a change.

(490 words)

 Vocabulary

1. treatment	n. 待遇，對待，處理，治療
2. consideration	n. 體諒，考慮
3. happily	adv. 幸福地，愉快地
4. prejudice	n. 偏見，成見
5. weaken	v. 削弱，（使）變弱
6. lib	n. (=liberation) 解放，釋放
7. consciousness	n. 意識，知覺，覺悟

8. recognize   vt. 認可，承認

9. acceptance   n. 接受，承諾，贊同

10. seriously   adv. 認真地，真誠地

11. Indiana   n. 印地安那州

12. in regard to   adv. 關於

📖 Useful Phrases and Expressions

1. a long way to go

2. Attention began to be paid to…

3. The story has usually been the same.

4. Consideration is given to…

5. Women have been thought of only as office workers.

6. People have a picture in their minds of…

7. The result has been that…

8. in most cases

9. prej udice against/to have prejudice against

10. The idea of liberation is becoming stronger.

11. consciousness-raising meetings

12. Women get together in small groups for…

13. This has led to…

14. in regard to

15. accept the fact that…

16. in short

17. be fighting to gain acceptance

18. Without question, women's lives are improving.

19. What you have here are a lot of happy women.

20. The idea is not taken seriously.

21. Do the work women are supposed to do.

22. Change may come slowly to...

 ## Exercises

I .Comprehension Questions

1. What used to be the prejudice against women? Give an example from the text.

2. When did the attitude towards women begin to change?

3. What made people change this attitude?

4. What do women in many countries like the United States and Canada do?

5. What do the women do at these meetings?

6. What has been the result of the women's liberation movement?

7. Do all women support the movement? Why?

8. What will the women's movement do?

II .Essay Writing

Write an essay by putting together the answers to the questions in Exercise I, using such joining words as because, and, but and so on.

III .Questions for Discussion

1. Do you think women's liberation movement is necessary? What are your points of view?

2. Is there any prejudice against women in our country? Is there a need to improve women's lives in our country?

IV .Translation

Put the following Chinese into English, using as many as possible the phrases and expressions you have learned.

1. 做你應當做的事。

2. 在接受你之前，公司一定會考慮你的學歷、自身條件和工作經驗。

3. 工安事件一直很被重視。討論勞工的人權問題以及他們的安全和福利 （well-being）。我們必須認真對待這一人群。現在社會上對他們還存在 不少偏見，很多城市尤其是一些大城市的人不願接受他們或把他們當做二 等公民。可是這些城裡人忘了這一人群對城市的經濟發展起著舉足輕重的 作用。

4. 長期以來，人們有很多不良習慣，但這些不良習慣一直沒有受到重視。直 到「SARS」發生後人們才逐漸開始重視這些陋習。從學校到街道，人們 聯合起來開會討論如何改掉這些不良習慣。在週末，學生到市中心、社區 去宣傳，告訴人們不要隨地吐痰（spit）和亂丟垃圾（litter）。結果現在 吐痰和亂扔垃圾的人越來越少了。

Lesson 11 Chicago Unblocks Traffic

Commuting to work in Chicago is no pleasure, for the roads there are even more crowded than in San Francisco. But here is how the city of Chicago is handling the problem.

"We don't have rush hours any more," said Charles M.McLean, who runs the nation's busiest road. "We have rush periods, and they keep getting longer and longer."

McLean was describing Chicago's 235 miles of expressway, especially the Kennedy Expressway. But the same might be said about almost any of the expressways that have become an important part of American city life—and about the heavy traffic that often blocks them.

In Chicago, a computerized system has been developed that controls traffic on the city's seven expressways. Now, one man—a controller—can follow the movement of Chicago's traffic by looking at a set of lights.

The system uses electronic sensors that are built into each expressway, half a mile apart. Several times a second, the computer receives information from each sensor and translates it into green, yellow, or red lights on a map in the control room.

A green light means traffic is moving forty-five to sixty miles an hour, yellow means thirty to forty-five miles an hour, and red means heavy traffic—cars standing still or moving less than thirty miles an hour.

"See that red light near Austin Avenue?" the controller asked a visitor. "That's a repair truck fixing the road, and the traffic has to go around it."

At the Roosevelt Road entrance to the expressway, the light kept changing from green to red and back to green again. "A lot of trucks get on the expressway there," the controller explained. "They can't speed up as fast as cars."

The sensors show immediately where an accident or a stopped car is blocking traffic, and a truck is sent by radio to clear the road. The system has lowered accidents by 18 percent. There are now 1.4 deaths on Chicago's expressways for each one hundred million miles traveled, while nationally there are 2.6.

Traffic experts say that the Chicago system is the "coming thing". Systems like Chicago's are already in use on some expressways in Los Angeles and Houston. "Chicago has taken the lead," says New York City's traffic director; and he adds, "we are far behind."

(390 words)

 Vocabulary

1. Chicago	n. 芝加哥（美國中西部大城市）
2. unblock	vt. 除去障礙
3. commute	v. 乘車上下班，交換
4. San Francisco	n. 舊金山
5. expressway	n. 高速道路
6. computerize	vt. 用計算機處理，使計算機化
7. electronic	adj. 電子的
8. sensor	n. 傳感器
9. nationally	adv. 全國性地，舉國一致地
10. expert	n. 專家，行家

11. Los Angeles   n. 洛杉磯（美國城市）

12. Houston   n. 休斯頓

 Useful Phrases and Expressions

1. Commuting to work in Chicago is no pleasure.

2. handle the problem

3. We don't have rush hours any more. We have rush periods and they keep getting longer and longer.

4. The same might be said about...

5. Expressways have become an important part of American city life.

6. A controller can follow the movement of Chicago's traffic by looking at a set of lights.

7. The system uses electronic sensors.

8. Cars stand still.

9. A repair truck is fixing the road and the traffic has to go around it.

10. A stopped car is blocking traffic.

11. clear the road

12. The system has lowered accidents by 18(%) percent.

13. Traffic experts say that the Chicago system is the coming thing.

14. Chicago has taken the lead.

15. 1 We are far behind...

 Exercises

I .Comprehension Questions

1. Why is it not a pleasure to commute to work in Chicago?

2. How crowded is the city of Chicago?

3. How is the overcrowding problem handled?

4. What is so good about this computerized system?

5. How does it work?

6. What do the traffic experts say about this system?

II .Essay Writing

Write an essay by putting together the answers to the questions in Exercise I, using such joining words as because, and, but and so on.

III .Discussion Questions

1. How do you think of this computerized system for traffic control? What are your reasons?

2. Can we borrow this idea to improve traffic situation in our big cities?

IV .Translation

Put the following Chinese into English, using as many as possible the phrases and expressions you have learned.

1. 很多外國人都不敢在曼谷、吉隆坡等大城市開車。不管他們的車有多好，在曼谷、吉隆坡開車絕不是一種享受。

2. 全世界沒有幾個大城市能夠解決交通擁擠問題，但波士頓（Boston）是個例外。它採取了徹底解決的辦法（once for all），把市中心的交通轉入地下，在地下建立一個完全由電腦控制的交通系統。波士頓是個中等城市（medium-sized），人口有 57 萬，到處都是具有歷史價值的建築。在 1950 年代這裡建築了一條穿過市中心的快速路。這條路剛修成時的確起了很大的作用，改善了城市交通擁擠的狀況。可是，到了 80 年代它卻成了全市最擠的路。每天要塞車 8 小時，交通事故頻頻發生。於是市政府決心徹底解決這一大問題。

　　這項工程在 1991 年開工，於 2004 年完成。地下公路很寬，雙向八車道（8 lanes for dual traffic），通向四面八方，有些地方和地鐵相通。地下沒有紅綠燈，車速很快，每小時平均 50 ～ 60 英里。交通流量（traffic flow）比地面加快了三倍。交通專家說，發展地下交通是個趨勢，波士頓給我們開了一個好頭。

Lesson 12　Life in a New Country

Mike and Jean are newly married. They had been told by their friends about the interesting opportunities in Japan. They decided to move to Japan and wanted to earn good salaries at their jobs. Both of them had a good educational background. Mike had been an engineer and Jean had been a teacher but she had studied management and business procedures in New York State University. They were excited about living in a different culture.

When they moved to Japan everything was new and strange. At first, things were not easy. Mike and Jean didn't have any friends in Japan. No housing arrangement had been made for them before they came. They had to find one quickly. They found a small furnished apartment, but it was very expensive. Their neighbours, the Takadas, were very friendly and gave them a lot of help. The Takadas, who could speak English, helped Mike and Jean improve their Japanese and understand Japanese culture. Mrs.Takada often helped Jean with her shopping.

Mike soon got a job with a Japanese electronics company but Jean was not as lucky as her husband. She hoped to get a job with a Japanese business company but it wasn't easy. She was sure she could be successful but had to be patient. One day Jean went for an interview with a large exporting company. Mr.Sobata, the owner of the company, needed someone to teach English to some of his employees. At first Jean was a bit nervous and afraid that she might not get the job. However, Mr.Sobata was very interested in Jean's qualifications and was very much impressed by her understanding of Japanese culture and language. At the end of the interview he told her to come and start the next day.

Now, both are earning good salaries. They have moved to a bigger and nicer house. They have some friends and some of them are Japanese and others are American and British. They often visit the Takadas, who are their closest friends. Life in a new country can be hard, but it can be very exciting.

(351 words)

 Vocabulary

1.	newly	adv. 重新，最近，以新的方式
2.	married	adj. 已婚的，婚姻的
3.	opportunity	n. 機會，時機
4.	decide	adj. 決定
5.	salary	n. 薪水／vt. 給…加薪
6.	background	n. 背景，後臺
7.	management	n. 經營，管理，處理；操縱
8.	procedure	n. 程序，手續
9.	culture	n. 文化，文明
10.	housing	n. 供給住宅，住房供給
11.	arrangement	n. 排列，安排
12.	quickly	adv. 很快地
13.	furnish	vt. 供應，提供，裝備，布置
14.	apartment	n. ＜美＞公寓住宅，單位住宅
15.	electronics	n. 電子學
16.	company	n. 公司
17.	interview	n. 接見，會見；面試

18. export   v. 輸出，出口

19. employee   n. 職工，僱員，店員

20. qualification   n. 資格，條件，限制

21. 2 impress   vt. 印，蓋印；留下印象

 Useful Phrases and Expressions

1. Mike and Jean are newly married.

2. interesting opportunities

3. earn good salaries at their jobs

4. education background

5. study management and business procedures

6. They were excited about doing something.

7. Everything was new and strange.

8. Things were not easy.

9. housing arrangement (to make housing arrangement)

10. furnished apartment

11. Mike got a job with a Japanese electronics company.

12. be patient

13. go for an interview with

14. be nervous

15. be very impressed by

16. at the end of

17. Life in a new country can be hard, but it can be very exciting.

Exercises

I .Comprehension Questions

1. Who are Mike and Jean?

2. Why did they want to move to Japan?

3. What did they do before they moved to Japan?

4. What education background did they have?

5. What did Jean hope to do?

6. How were things when they first arrived in Japan?

7. What difficulties did they have?

8. Did they get any help from someone? Who?

9. How did things work out later?

10. Are they happy now in Japan?

II .Essay Writing

Write an essay by putting together the answers to the questions in Exercise I, using such joining words as because, and, but and so on.

III .Questions for Discussion

1. Why did Mike and Jean want to move to Japan? Apart from financial reason, can you think of some other reasons? Can you understand this newly married couple?

2. Do you wish to live in a new country? What country would you like to live in? Why?

IV.Translation

Put the following Chinese into English, using as many as possible the phrases and expressions you have learned.

　　趙勇夫 23 歲，剛從台灣大學電腦工程（computer science）系畢業。他決定去台東一個新發電廠（power plant）工作。在學校時他當了三年學生會主席，並且學業一直表現優異。按他的學歷和條件很容易在台北或其他國外大城市找一份薪資優厚的工作。他要去台東工作的原因很簡單，他說國家正計畫開發東部，那裡很需要像他這樣的人才。作為一名受過良好教育的青年，他深感自己應當為國家做些工作。他知道剛開始時會有很多困難，人生地不熟，但他不在乎。相反，他對要去一個跟家鄉完全不同的城市工作覺得很興奮。他的父母親認為他這決定做得好，為他感到驕傲。再過兩星期他就要啟程去台東了。他對他的朋友說，好的機遇在等著他，一定不能錯過。他堅信他會很成功的。

Lesson 13 In a Bookshop

Time spent in a bookshop can be most enjoyable, whether you are a book-lover or merely there to buy a book as a present. You may even have entered the shop just to find shelter from a sudden shower. Whatever the reason, you can soon become totally unaware of your surroundings. You soon become engrossed in some book or other, and usually it is only much later that you realize you have spent too much time there and must dash off to keep some forgotten appointment.

This opportunity to escape the realities of everyday life is the main attraction of a bookshop. A music shop is very much like a bookshop. You can wander round such places to your heart's content. If it is a good shop, no assistant will approach you with the inevitable greeting, "Can I help you?". You needn't buy anything you don't want. In a bookshop an assistant should remain in the background until you have finished browsing. Then, and only then, are his services necessary.

Once a medical student had to read a textbook which was far too expensive for him to buy. He couldn't obtain it from the library and the only copy he could find was in a certain bookshop. Every afternoon, therefore, he would go along to the shop and read a little of the book at a time. One day, however, he was disappointed to find the book missing from its usual place. He was about to leave, when he noticed the owner of the shop beckoning to him. Expecting to be told off, he went towards him. To his surprise, the owner pointed to the book which was tucked away in a corner. "I put it there in case anyone was tempted to buy it!" he said, and left the delighted student to continue his reading.

(310 words)

Vocabulary

1. enjoyable	adj. 令人愉快的，可享受的
2. shelter	n. 掩蔽處，掩蔽，保護；庇護所
3. totally	adv. 完全地，整全地
4. unaware	adj. 不知道的，沒覺察到的
5. surroundings	n. 環境
6. engross	vt. 吸引，使全神貫注
7. appointment	n. 約會，指定
8. reality	n. 真實，事實
9. everyday	adj. 每天的，日常的，平常的
10.attraction	n. 吸引，吸引力，吸引人的事物
11.wander	vi. 漫步，徘徊
12.content	n. 滿足
13.inevitable	adj. 不可避免的
14.obtain	vt. 獲得，得到
15.missing	adj. 不見的，缺少的
16.beckon	v. 招手，召喚
17.tuck	vt. 擠進，塞；使隱藏
18.tempt	vt. 誘惑，引誘，吸引
19.in case	萬一

 Useful Phrases and Expressions

1. Time spent in a bookshop can be enjoyable.

2. book-lover

3. find shelter from a sudden shower

4. become totally unaware of your surroundings

5. dash off to keep some forgotten appointment

6. escape the realities of everyday life

7. the main attraction of

8. wander round such places to your heart's content

9. remain in the background

10. far too expensive for him to buy

11. read a little of the book at a time

12. find the book missing from his usual place

13. He was about to leave when...

14. be told off

15. to his surprise

16. tuck away something in

17. He left the student to continue his reading.

 Exercises

I .Comprehension Questions

1. Why is it that time spent in a bookshop can be most enjoyable?

2. What is the main attraction of a bookshop?

3. Do you have to buy anything in a bookshop?

4. Will the shop assistant bother you?

5. What happened to a medical student?

6. What did he do to solve his problem?

7. Why did he feel disappointed one day?

8. What happened to the book?

9. What did the owner of the bookshop tell the student?

10. What did the owner do after that?

II .Essay Writing

Write an essay by putting together the answers to the questions in Exercise I, using such joining words as because, and, but and so on.

III .Questions for Discussion

1. Do you share the same idea with the writer that time spent in a bookshop can be most enjoyable? What are your reasons?

2. Do you think the story in the text about the owner of a bookshop is true? Why do you think so? What do you think of the owner?

IV .Translation

Put the following Chinese into English, using as many as possible the phrases and expressions you have learned.

　　暑假一開始，我和我老婆就去了黃山。以前我聽說過很多有關黃山的故事，可是一直沒有機會去。在念書時，我就很想去黃山，但是費用太高沒去成。遊玩黃山一般需 1～2 天，我們玩了五天。一個原因是為了避暑，另一個原因是為了好好看看黃山。以後我們不太有機會再去了，因此，不想漏掉任何好玩的地方。黃山最吸引人的是它美麗又雄偉的自然風光（magnificent natural scenery）。我們每到一處都可見到奇形怪狀的岩石和高大的松樹。黃山的松樹和其他地方的松樹不一樣。每天早上我們六點起床，起床後就坐在飯店前觀賞奇特的樹和岩石，很快我們就陶醉在美麗的晨色中。早飯後我們就到處走走，直到我們心滿意足為止。最後一天，我們去遊覽一個峽谷。由於雲太多什麼都看不見，我們感到有些失望。當我們要返回時，突然下起雨來，我們馬上跑到附近的山洞裡避雨。沒多久雨就停了。我們走出山洞時，看到又深又綠的峽谷很驚訝。我們從未見過那麼迷人的景色。那次去黃山玩得真是盡興。

Lesson 14　Public Transport

Nearly every major city in the world provides some form of public transport. This is necessary not only for visitors to the city, but also to provide citizens with low-cost transport and to help the traffic on the streets and highways.

The most common form of public transport is the bus. Buses have been in use in major cities since about 1900. They provide transport service on innumerable routes from the city center to the suburbs and even to outlying rural areas that surround the city. Also, special buses can be hired for trips to mountains, to lakes, and to nearby places of historical interest. In some cities, the city bus system offers a free "mini-bus" service as a convenience to shoppers in the downtown business district.

Subways are mostly found in larger cities, such as New York, London, Paris, Beijing, Moscow and Tokyo. The subway is in an underground system of high-speed trains. The world's first system was built in London, and trains have been operating there since 1890. Subway trains move more quickly and efficiently than buses. They take you to almost any place in the city. They, too, are inexpensive and help solve city traffic problems. The one drawback of subway trains is that they are often crowded and noisy.

Taxicabs are more expensive than buses and subways, but they will take you to the exact destination you want in the shortest possible time. Taxis are convenient if you are in a hurry or if you are taking along a number of suitcases or baggage. And as an added attraction, many cab drivers will tell you stories about their adventures as a taxicab driver or even the details of their life stories.

If you ever visit a big city in another country, you will probably have no trouble getting around. You will quickly find out about city bus routes and schedules, of subway trains, and probably, about the scarcity of taxis when you are trying to find one during rush hours. Like many people, of course, you may come to the conclusion that the most inexpensive and reliable form of transport will be your own two legs!

(356 words)

 Vocabulary

1. transport	n. 運輸
2. highway	n. 公路，大路
3. innumerable	adj. 無數的，數不清的
4. route	n. 路線，路程，通道
5. suburb	n. 市郊，郊區
6. outlying	adj. 邊遠的，偏僻的
7. rural	adj. 鄉下的，生活在農村的
8. surround	vt. 包圍，環境
9. nearby	adj. 附近的，鄰近的
10. historical	adj. 歷史（上）的，有關歷史的
11. mini-	n. [前綴] 小的
12. downtown	adj. 市區的
13. subway	n. 地道，＜美＞地鐵
14. mostly	adv. 主要地，大部分，通常
15. London	n. 倫敦

16. Paris	n. 巴黎（法國首都）
17. Moscow	n. 莫斯科（俄羅斯首都）
18. Tokyo	n. 東京（日本首都）
19. underground	adj. 地下的，地面下的
20. efficiently	adv. 有效率地，有效地
21. inexpensive	adj. 便宜的，不貴重的
22. drawback	n. 劣勢
23. taxicab	n. 計程車
24. destination	n. 目的地
25. baggage	n. 行李
26. cab	n. 計程汽車，計程車
27. detail	n. 細節，詳情
28. schedule	n. 時間表，進度表
29. scarcity	n. 缺乏，不足
30. conclusion	n. 結論
31. reliable	adj. 可靠的，可信賴的

 Useful Phrases and Expressions

1. This is necessary for...

2. provide citizens with low-cost transport

3. help reduce the traffic on streets and highways

4. Buses have been in use in major cities since...

5. outlying rural areas

6. city bus system

7. offer free mini-bus service as a convenience to shoppers

8. Subways are mostly found in larger cities.

9. Trains have been operating since...

10. The one drawback of subway trains is that...

11. 1 in the shortest possible time

12. have no trouble getting around

13. 1 You will quickly find out about...

14. come to the conclusion that...

 Exercises

I .Comprehension Questions

1. What does every big city provide? Why?

2. What is the most common form of public transport?

3. How long have buses been in use in major cities?

4. Where can you find subways?

5. When and where was the world's first subway built?

6. What is the advantage of the subway?

7. Does it have any drawback? What is it?

8. Are taxicabs more expensive?

9. What are the good things about taxi?

10. Why is it that if you visit a big city you will have no trouble getting around the city?

11. What is the most inexpensive and reliable form of transport when you are in a city?

II .Essay Writing

Write an essay by putting together the answers to the questions in Exercise I, using such joining words as because, and, but and so on.

III .Questions for Discussion

1. Why is it that a good and efficient public transport system is extremely important to big cities?

2. China is a country with a huge population, and there are many big cities. What do you think is the best form of public transport? Why?

IV .Translation

Put the following Chinese into English, using as many as possible the phrases and expressions you have learned.

德國的城市公共交通是世界聞名的。大眾運輸形式有好幾種，最普遍的是火車。由於越來越多的人搬到遠郊或遠離大城市的地方去居住，快捷高效的軌道交通就成為一種必不可少的運輸方式。實際上，在德國高速火車從 1980 年起一直在運行。火車的特點是準時、舒適和高效。火車載客遠遠比公共汽車多。絕大部分火車站同地鐵和公共汽車相連。火車票制很有特色，票的種類很多，如有年票、季票、月票、日票，還有全國通用的票。票價不貴，在售票機上就可買到票，所有的車站裡都有售票機。

德國的大眾交通服務是一流的。差不多所有的火車站、地鐵站、公共汽車站都有問訊處。工作人員可隨時回答乘客的問題和提供幫助。而且他們都能講好幾種外語。地圖、時刻表都是免費的。有些火車站還為旅客提供汽車租賃服務。旅客到站後可自己駕車遊玩。如果旅客要帶自己的汽車或自行車，車站可提供服務。當然，要收服務費。

德國的計程車在歐洲是有口皆碑的，但貴一點。計程車大、乾淨、舒適。如果你要坐計程車的話，只需打個電話給計程車公司，五分鐘後計程車就會到，司機會在最短的時間內安全地把你送到目的地。德國計程車司機穿戴整潔，有禮貌、耐心、和氣，助人為樂。難怪外國遊客都會感到在德國乘坐計程車是一種享受呢。

Lesson 15　A Short Autobiography

I was born in a big business center in my country. I am twentysix now. I am the second child in the family. I have a brother who is two years older than me. When I was still very small, my father died after a long sickness. Then, the whole family moved to the capital city where my grandparents lived. My mother's training as an accountant soon helped her get a job with the Ministry of Finance. But she earned just enough to keep our heads above water. After I completed my elementary education in a public school near our house, I attended a good middle school.

In the middle school I began to develop a special interest in biology and horticulture, the study of flowers and fruit trees. In addition, I took courses in chemistry, maths, and economics along with laboratory courses. In the lab we did experiments with plants and trees and studied irrigation, insect control and harvesting techniques. Apart from my academic interests, I was fond of music and I was the lead guitarist in a school musical group. We played music for student activities and local clubs. At one time I was considering taking up music as a career.

Then, I went on to study biology in one of the best universities in the country. After I finished university, I went to work for a large agricultural company. I have been with the company for two years. My main responsibility is to supervise the fruit production. I have to make sure everything from planning to irrigation methods is done correctly. I love my job and I have been quite successful. Now I have already established myself in the company.

Next year, my company will be sending me to Cambridge in England to study for a Master's degree. Before going I decided to take a six-month English course because my English is not adequate enough to study in England. When I finish my Master's degre, I will return to my company, and I will be put in a more important position.

I have several other interests in addition to music. I love meeting people and enjoy traveling. As a matter of fact, traveling around the world will be part of my future work. I enjoy adventure movies and hardly miss any new adventure movies.

I am looking forward eagerly to my new life in England. I am quite confident that I will learn a lot about my field in Cambridge. And I am sure I will certainly meet many interesting people there. During the holidays I will travel to interesting places in Britain. Of course I can still find time to play my guitar.

(446 words)

 Vocabulary

1.	autobiography	n. 自傳
2.	sickness	n. 疾病，嘔吐
3.	grandparent	n. 祖父母
4.	accountant	n. 會計（員），會計師
5.	ministry	n.（政府的）部門
6.	finance	n. 財政，金融，財政學
7.	elementary	adj. 初步的，基本的
8.	biology	n. 生物學，生物（總稱）
9.	horticulture	n. 園藝
10.	maths	n. 數學
11.	economics	n. 經濟學

12. irrigation   n. 灌溉，沖洗

13. insect   n. 昆蟲

14. apart   adj. 分開的

15. academic   adj. 學院的，理論的

16. guitarist   n. 吉他彈奏者

17. activity   n. 活躍，活動性，行動，行為

18. local   adj. 地方的，當地的，局部的，鄉土的

19. career   n. 事業，生涯

20. responsibility   n. 責任，職責

21. supervise   v. 監督，管理，指導

22. correctly   adv. 恰當地，正確地

23. establish   vt. 建立，設立，安置

24. adequate   adj. 適當的，足夠的

25. eagerly   adv. 熱心地，急切地

26. Britain   n. 英國

27. guitar   n. 吉他，六絃琴

 Useful Phrases and Expressions

1. I am the second child.

2. My father died after long sickness.

3. My mother's training as an accountant soon helped her get a job.

4. after I completed my elementary education

5. develop a special interest in...

6. in addition/in addition to

7. I took courses in...along with laboratory courses.

8. insect control

9. harvesting techniques

10. Apart from my academic interests, I was fond of...

11. I was the lead guitarist.

12. At one time I was considering taking up music as a career.

13. I went to work for a large agricultural company.

14. I have been with the company for...

15. My main responsibility is to

16. I have been quite successful.

17. I have already established myself in the company.

18. My English is not adequate enough to...

19. I will be put in a more important position.

20. Visiting around the world will be part of my future work.

21. I hardly miss any new adventure movies.

22. I am looking forward eagerly to...

23. I am quite confident that...

 Exercises

I .Comprehension Questions

1. How old is the narrator（講述人）?

2. What happened when she was still very small?

3. What did his family do after her father died?

4. Did her mother get a job in the new city?

5. Did her mother earn a lot of money? How much did she earn?

6. After her primary education what did the narrator do?

7. What interest did she develop in the middle school?

8. Did she have any other interest?

9. Was she a good guitarist? How good was she?

10. Did she go on to university after middle school?

11. What did she study in university?

12. Did she have a job after university? Where?

13. What did she do in the company? Was she successful?

14. What is her company going to do next year?

15. What did she decide to do before going to England?

16. What does she plan to do after she gets a Master's degree?

17. Will she do the same job after she returns to the company?

18. Is she a person with many interests?

19. What is she looking forward to now?

II .Essay Writing

Write an essay by putting together the answers to the questions in Exercise I, using such joining words as because, and, but and so on.

III .Questions for Discussion

1. What country is the narrator from? Why do you think so?

2. Do you want to have a friend like the narrator? Why?

3. Write a short autobiography of yourself

IV .Translation

Put the following Chinese into English, using as many as possible the phrases and expressions you have learned.

陳東今年 30 歲，出生在台北一個富裕家庭裡。他的父親是位成功的商人。他剛出生不久，父親就拋棄他們母子倆去了義大利，從此杳無音信。第二年，母子倆就搬到新北市附近一個小鄉鎮跟他的外祖父母一起住。為了養家，他的母親不得不外出找工作。由於她受過很好的教育，在一所中學裡謀到一個職位，但工資很少，只能勉強維持生活。

陳東念的高中在這小鎮裡是最好的。學習期間，他一直是全班第一名，三年中從未缺過課。在中學裡他對化學產生了興趣。中學畢業後，被台大大學化學系錄取。他聰明刻苦，四年的課程他三年就完成了，然後被學校送去攻讀碩士學位。他提前一年拿到了碩士學位，並繼續攻讀博士學位。26 歲時他拿到了博士學位。取得博士學位後，學校請他留校任教和做科學研究。他很快在工作中立足並被大家承認。

除了教學，他還負責實驗室的一項關於控制愛滋病的研究項目。另外他還忙於一項預防「SARS」的新項目。他在研究工作方面一直很出色，現在是台灣大學主要的研究員之一。他堅信在不久的將來會有一種預防「SARS」的藥問世。

Lesson 16   People and Oceans

The oceans cover more than seventy percent of the earth's surface. The Pacific, Atlantic, Indian, Arctic, and Antarctic Oceans are really one large body of water broken by the islands that we call continents. Although people have been studying the oceans for many years, there is still much that we do not know about them. Today, oceanographers are looking for new ways to use the ocean.

The ocean has always been used as a source of food. Each year, the world's fishing industry catches billions of kilograms of fish. The fishing industry, however, produces only a small percentage of the world's food. Oceanographers are seeking ways to increase the amount of food taken from the ocean. Many undersea plants contain vitamins and minerals. Perhaps in the future, people will be able to grow these plants on undersea farms.

The ocean can also provide a source of energy. Scientists have been trying to develop ways to use the energy of the ocean's tides to produce electric power. The world's first tidal power plant was built in France and began operating in 1996. However, new technology is needed to make tidal power plants more efficient. The ocean is also becoming a major source of oil. Many oil wells have been dug beneath the ocean, but some of them have caused environmental problems.

People have also been dumping waste into the sea. In some cities, barges carry garbage, industrial waste, and other materials out to sea and dump them in the ocean. The ocean cannot hold too much of these things without endangering its fish and plants. As the world population increases, people will need more products from the sea. Everyone must work to protect these products by keeping the oceans free from pollution.

(267 words)

Vocabulary

1.	Pacific	n. [the P~] 太平洋
2.	Atlantic	n. 大西洋
3.	arctic	n. 北極，北極圈
4.	Antarctic	adj. 南極的
5.	continent	n. 大陸，陸地
6.	oceanographer	n. 海洋學者，海洋研究者
7.	source	n. 來源，水源；消息來源；原始資料
8.	fishing	n. 釣魚，捕魚
9.	percentage	n. 百分數，百分率，百分比
10.	amount	n. 數量
11.	undersea	adj. 海面下的，海底的
12.	vitamin	n. 維他命，維生素
13.	tide	n. 潮，潮汐；潮流，趨勢
14.	efficient	adj. 有效率的，能幹的
15.	beneath	prep. 在……之下
16.	environmental	adj. 周圍的，環境的
17.	barge	n. 駁船，遊艇／vt. 用船運輸
18.	garbage	n. 垃圾，廢物
19.	industrial	adj. 工業的，產業的，實業的
20.	dump	vt. 傾倒（垃圾），傾卸
21.	endanger	vt. 危及

22. keeping   n. 保守，看守，遵守

23. pollution   n. 汙染

 Useful Phrases and Expressions

1. The oceans cover more than seventy percent of the earth's surface.

2. There is still much that we do not know about them.

3. Oceanographers are looking for new ways to use the ocean.

4. The ocean has always been used as a source of food.

5. Oceanographers are seeking ways to increase the amount of...

6. The ocean can also provide a source of energy.

7. develop ways to use the energy of the ocean's tides

8. tidal power plant

9. begin operating

10. New technology is needed to make... more efficient.

11. 1 cause environmental problems

12. The ocean cannot hold too much of these things.

13. 1 dump waste into the sea

14. Everyone must work to protect... by keeping the oceans free from pollution.

 Exercises

I .Comprehension Questions

1. Why do we say that the ocean has always been a source of food?

2. What other thing can we get from the ocean?

3. How do we use the ocean to get energy?

4. When and where was the first tidal power plant put into use?

5. What is needed to make tidal power plants more efficient?

6. What another energy source can the ocean provide for people?

7. What is the problem with this energy source?

8. As the ocean is so important to people, do they take good care of it? What are the facts?

9. What must people do to the ocean?

II .Essay Writing

Write an essay by putting together the answers to the questions in Exercise I, using such joining words as because, and, but and so on.

III .Questions for Discussion

1.What do you think is the relation between people and the ocean? Why do you think so?

2.Why is it that people do not take good care of the ocean?

IV .Translation

Put the following Chinese into English, using as many as possible the phrases and expressions you have learned.

三峽水利工程是世界之最。整個長江三峽就是個水庫（reservoir）。這個水利工程的作用很大，它可以防洪，保護長江沿岸的城市農村免受洪澇災害。目前水庫的水位（water level）是 135 公尺，水庫還能蓄更多的水。這個水利工程全部完成後，水位將達 175 公尺，那時萬噸輪船可輕而易舉地從上海直達重慶。水路運輸是最經濟的。當水位達 175 公尺時，三峽水力發電廠（hydro-electric power plant）的 26 臺機組（electric generators）可全部發電，年發電量可達 850 億千瓦（kilowatts），可供很多省市使用。水力發電無汙染，對環保有益（environment-friendly）。此外，三峽工程還促進了長江三峽的旅遊業，因為三峽有很多新的景點可供人們遊覽。

Lesson 17　Changing Eating Habits

In 1955, a man named Raymond Kroc, together with two brothers named McDonald, operated a popular restaurant in California which sold food that was easy to prepare and serve quickly. Hamburgers, French fries, and cold drinks were the main items on the limited menu. Kroc opened similar eating places under the same name, "McDonald's" and they were an instant success. He later took over the company, and today it is one of the most famous and successful "fast food" chains in America and the world.

Why was his idea so successful? Probably the most significant reason was that his timing was right. In the 1950s, most married women stayed at home to keep house and take care of their children. During the decade of the 1960s, the movement for equality between the sexes and an economy that required more families to have two wage-earners resulted in many women returning to the work place. This meant they had less time and energy to do housework and prepare meals, so they relied more on "TV dinners" and fast-food restaurants.

Single parents also have little time to spend in the kitchen. Convenience foods, processed and packaged, help a great deal. People living alone because of divorce or a preference for a simple lifestyle also depend on this type of food, since cooking for one is often more trouble than it is worth. Food manufacturers have begun catering to this new market and now sell smaller portions specially prepared for just one person.

Fast food, or junk food as it is sometimes called, is not part of the diet of all Americans. Another trend of the 1960s, sometimes called the back-to-nature movement or the hippie movement, influenced many people to avoid food that was packaged or processed. More and more Americans based their diets on natural foods containing no chemicals such as additives, preservatives, or artificial colors or flavors. This preference for natural foods continues to this day. These products can now be found not only in the special health food stores but also on the shelves of many supermarkets.

The success of Raymond Kroc's fast-food business and the increasing interest in natural foods are illustrations of the way in which social and economical trends influence where and what we eat.

(376 words)

Vocabulary

1.	California	n. 加利福尼亞，加州
2.	hamburger	n. ＜美＞漢堡
3.	french fries	n. 炸薯條
4.	item	n.（可分類或列舉的）項目，條款
5.	limited	adj. 有限的，狹窄的
6.	instant	adj. 立即的，即時的
7.	significant	adj. 有意義的，重大的，重要的
8.	decade	n. 十年，十
9.	equality	n. 等同性，同等，平等，相等
10.	economy	n. 經濟，節約；經濟制度的狀況
11.	wage	n. 工資
12.	rely	vi. 依賴，依靠，信賴，信任
13.	convenience	n. 便利，方便，有益

14. process　　　vt. 加工，處理

15. package　　　vt. 包裝，打包

16. divorce　　　n. 離婚；脫離

17. preference　　n. 偏愛，優先選擇

18. lifestyle　　　n. 生活方式

19. manufacturer　n. 製造業者，廠商

20. cater　　　　vi. 備辦食物；滿足（需要），投合

21. portion　　　n. 一部分，一份

22. specially　　　adv. 特別地

23. junk　　　　n. 垃圾

24. diet　　　　　n. 通常所吃的食物

25. trend　　　　n. 傾向，趨勢

26. hippie　　　　n. 嬉皮

27. influence　　　vt. 影響，改變

28. avoid　　　　vt. 避免，消除

29. chemical　　　n. 化學製品，化學藥品

30. additive　　　n. 添加劑

31. preservative　n. 防腐劑

32. artificial　　　adj. 人造的，假的

33. flavor　　　　n. 風味，滋味，香料

34. product　　　n. 產品，產物

35. shelve　　　　vt. 置於架子上

36. illustration　　n. 說明，例證，例子

37. social   adj. 社會的，愛交際的，社交的

38. economical   adj. 節約的，經濟的

39. economic   adj. 經濟（上）的，經濟學的

 Useful Phrases and Expressions

1. Someone operates a popular restaurant in...

2. The restaurant sells food that is easy to prepare and serve quickly.

3. under the same name

4. They were an instant success.

5. He later took over the company.

6. fast-food chains

7. Probably the most significant reason was that his timing was right.

8. married women/men

9. stay home to keep house and take care of their children

10. wage-earners

11. result in many women returning to the workplace

12. This meant they had less time and energy to do housework.

13. single parent

14. convenience food stores

15. Cooking for one is often more trouble than it is worth.

16. back-to-nature movement

17. base their diets on natural foods

18. continue to this day

 **Exercises**

I .Comprehension Questions

1. When did Raymond Kroc and two brothers named McDonald operate a popular restaurant?

2. What did the restaurant sell?

3. What did Kroc do after that?

4. What was an instant success?

5. What was the main reason of Kroc's success?

6. What was another trend in the 1960s last century?

7. What do these changes in people's diets show?

II .Essay Writing

Write an essay by putting together the answers to the questions in Exercise I, using such joining words as because, and, but and so on.

III .Questions for Discussion

1. Do you find the same rule in China when social and economic changes cause people to change their diets? Give examples.

2. Are there any problems in our people's diet? Can we let this problem go on? How are we going to solve the problems?

IV .Translation

Put the following Chinese into English, using as many as possible the phrases and expressions you have learned.

Harlaved Sander 生活在美國肯德基州（kentucky）一個小鎮上。年輕時他做過很多工作，但沒有賺多少錢。40 歲那年，他在公路邊開了一家加油站（petrol station）。每天很多卡車在他那兒加油。不少司機開了很長時間的車感覺很餓，要吃東西，因此他就開了一個小餐館，供應好做而客人又不必等的食品。食膳很簡單，只有三明治、炸雞和咖啡。他那兒的食品好吃而不貴，所以在他那裡停下來的司機越來越多。他做的炸雞特別香，很多人都從很遠的地方開車來品嚐。

然而，一條新的公路建成了，大部分的卡車、轎車都去走新路了。餐館沒有生意只好關門。有一天，他突然想出一個主意：他要開很多專賣炸雞的小餐館，而雞的味道都是一樣的。他的想法是讓人們在一家能吃到的炸雞，在其他地方也可以吃到同樣的炸雞。由於他的炸雞味道好，這個想法得到很多人的支持。於是他就開始經營店名為「肯德基（Kentucky）」的連鎖店。那時他已 65 歲了。現在「肯德基（Kentucky）」炸雞分店遍布世界各地，2017 年 10 月為止，肯德基在台灣共有 137 家門市。

Lesson 18   Robots

Robots are becoming increasingly popular in factories and industrial plants throughout the developed world. They are designed to perform different kinds of jobs that are often boring and sometimes dangerous. Most of today's robots are employed in industry, where they are programmed to take over such assembly line operations as welding and spray painting automobile and truck bodies. They also load and unload hot, heavy metal forms used in machines. In addition, they install bulbs in instrument panels.

Robots build electric motors, small appliances, typewriters, pocket calculators, and even watches. The robots used in nuclear power plants handle the radioactive materials so that workers are not exposed to radiation. Robots differ from automatic machines. After robots have completed one specific task, they can be reprogrammed by a computer to do another task. Automatic machines cannot do that and therefore are less versatile. They are built to perform only one task. Robots are more flexible and adaptable and usually more transportable than other machines.

The new generation of robots can see, touch, hear and think. Robots used in factories can pick out defective products. Scientists use robots to find minerals on the ocean floor or in deep areas of mines, which are too dangerous for humans to enter. In some developed countries robots work as gas station attendants, firefighters, housekeepers and security guards. The robot business is growing at a high speed. Anyone who wants to understand the industries of the future will have to know about the technology of robots.

(251 words)

Vocabulary

1.	robot	n. 機器人
2.	increasingly	adv. 日益，愈加
3.	boring	adj. 令人厭煩的
4.	assembly	n. 集合，裝配，集會
5.	weld	vt. 銲接／n. 銲接，焊縫
6.	spray	n. 噴霧，飛沫／vt. 噴射，噴濺
7.	automobile	n. <主美>汽車（=<英>motor car, car）
8.	unload	vi. 卸貨，退子彈
9.	install	vt. 安裝，安置
10.	bulb	n. 麟莖，球形物
11.	instrument	n. 工具，手段，器械，器具
12.	panel	n. 面板，嵌板，儀表板
13.	appliance	n. 用具，器具
14.	typewriter	n. 打字機
15.	calculator	n. 電腦，計算器
16.	nuclear	adj. <核>核子的，原子能的，核的
17.	handle	vt. 處理，操作
18.	radioactive	adj. 放射性的，有輻射能的
19.	expose	vt. 使暴露，受到，使曝光
20.	radiation	n. 輻射，放射，放射線，放射物
21.	differ	vi. 不一致，不同
22.	automatic	adj. 自動的，機械的

23. specific   adj. 詳細而精確的，明確的

24. reprogramme   v. 改編，程序重編

25. versatile   adj. 通用的，萬能的，多才多藝的，有多種技能的

26. flexible   adj. 易曲的，靈活的，能變形的

27. adaptable   adj. 能適應的，可修改的

28. transportable   adj. 可運輸的

29. defective   adj. 有缺陷的

30. attendant   n. 服務員

31. firefighter   n. 消防員

32. housekeeper   n. 主婦，女管家

33. security   n. 安全

34. technology   n. 工藝，科技，技術

Useful Phrases and Expressions

1. be becoming increasingly popular

2. Most of today's robots are employed in...

3. take over such assembly line operations as welding...

4. metal forms

5. radioactive materials

6. be (not) exposed to radiation

7. Robots differ from automatic machines...

8. Automatic machines are less versatile...

9. defective products

10. find minerals on the ocean floor

11.1 The robot business is growing at a high speed...

 Exercises

I .Comprehension Questions

1. What is getting increasingly popular in the developed countries?

2. What jobs do the robots perform?

3. Why do people want to use robots?

4. What is the big difference between robots and automatic machines?

5. How advanced are the new generation of robots?

II .Essay Writing

Write an essay by putting together the answers to the questions in Exercise I, using such joining words as because, and, but and so on.

III .Questions for Discussion

1. Do you think robots will make a lot of workers unemployed?

2. Do you think there will be one day when many people have robot housekeepers to look after their houses? Why?

IV .Translation

Put the following Chinese into English, using as many as possible the phrases and expressions you have learned.

十五六年前，智慧型手機剛出現。現在智慧型手機越來越普遍了。在城市裡，特別是大城市裡，九成以上的人都有智慧型手機，在大學裡絕大部分的學生都有智慧型手機，很多中小學生也有智慧型手機。智慧型手機行業像電腦行業一樣發展很快。現在的智慧型手機有很多功能，它們不僅可以打電話，也可做鬧鐘，可以上網，還能照相錄影，有計算的功能，同時還能做遙控器（remote control）來開關家中的門、空調和家電。它們集多樣東西於一體。新一代手機使人們的生活更加方便、高效了。可是這種手機有一個問題，就是太貴。但是專家們說，它們的價格一直降下來，很多人都買得起。

Lesson 19　Air Pollution

The dark smoke that comes out of stacks, burning dumps and trucks and cars contains tiny bits of chemical matter. Most of this chemical matter cannot be seen by human eyes. It causes the serious problem of air pollution. In many places it keeps us from seeing the sun and causes us to cough or makes us ill. Air pollution can spread from city to city. It even spreads from one country to another. Some northern European countries have had "black snow" from pollutants that have traveled through the air from other countries and have fallen with the snow. So air pollution is really a global problem.

There are health dangers from air pollution. Statistics show that air pollution in cities increases the risk of certain lung diseases such as emphysema, bronchitis and asthma. It can kill babies, old people and those who have respiratory diseases. In London, in 1952, four thousand people died in one week as a result of serious air pollution. In 1948, in the small town of Donora, Pennsylvania, twenty people died in a four-day period of bad air pollution. Scientists have found out that chemicals in the polluted air can cause changes in our cells. These changes may cause babies to be born with serious defects. Scientists also have learned that these chemicals we are apt to take into our bodies from air, water and food act together to affect our health and the way our bodies work. In order to keep healthy and live longer, we must keep air pollution under control.

Air pollution can cause airplane and auto accidents because it cuts down visibility. It also has harmful effects on animals, plants and farm crops. It damages our works of art and dirties and corrodes our fine buildings. The cost of all this damage in the United States is thought to be more than $20 billion every year. This is far more than the money we need to control air pollution. So air pollution is not only a big threat to our health but it also costs us a tremendous amount of money. That is another reason why we must find every possible way to control air pollution. Though it is still difficult now to solve the problem of air pollution completely, we cannot afford to wait till we have all the answers.

(375 words)

 Vocabulary

1. stack	n. 煙囪;堆,一堆
2. pollutant	n. 汙染物質
3. global	adj. 球形的,全球的,全世界的
4. statistics	n. 統計學,統計表
5. lung	n. 肺,肺臟
6. emphysema	n. 氣腫,肺氣腫
7. bronchitis	n. <醫> 支氣管炎
8. asthma	n. <醫> 哮喘
9. respiratory	adj. 呼吸的
10. pollute	vt. 弄髒,汙染
11. cell	n. 細胞
12. defect	n. 過失,缺點
13. apt	adj. 易於……的,有……傾向的
14. auto	n. <美><口> 汽車
15. visibility	n. 可見度,可見性,明顯度
16. damage	vt. 損害
17. corrode	v. 使腐蝕,侵蝕

18. threat   n. 恐嚇，凶兆，威脅

19. tremendous   adj. 極大的，巨大的

 Useful Phrases and Expressions

1. It keeps us from...

2. Air pollution can spread from city to city.

3. a global problem

4. respiratory diseases

5. Four thousand people died in one week in a four-day period.

6. Statistics show that...

7. Air pollution increases the risk of...

8. It cuts down visibility.

9. There are other possible health dangers from air pollution.

10. Something may cause changes in our cells.

11. babies born with serious defects

12. We are apt to take sth.into our bodies

13. ...act together to affect our health

14. That is another reason why it is so important to...

15. It has a destructive effect on our works of art.

16. The United States is thought to be...

 Exercises

I .Comprehension Questions

1. What makes up air pollution?

2. Where do these chemicals come from?

3. Why is air pollution a global problem?

4. Is air pollution dangerous to people's health? Why? Can you give an example from the text?

5. What have scientists found out about these chemicals?

6. What are the other harmful effects caused by air pollution?

7. How much money is thought to spend on the cost of all the damages done by air pollution in the United States?

8. Can we solve the problem of air pollution completely now?

9. What must we do then?

II .Essay Writing

Write an essay by putting together the answers to the questions in Exercise I, using such joining words as because, and, but and so on.

III .Questions for Discussion

1. Is the problem of air pollution in your city serious? What causes the problem? Give some facts.

2. What is your idea to solve the problem of air pollution in your city?

IV .Translation

Put the following Chinese into English, using as many as possible the phrases and expressions you have learned.

聯合國世界衛生組織（World Health Organization）說吸菸是個全球問題。這個問題每天都在惡化，在發展中國家尤為嚴重。吸菸對健康的危害很大，絕大部分呼吸道疾病和肺癌都是由吸煙引起的。據統計每年全球有三百萬人死於吸菸。這就意味著每 10 秒鐘有一人因吸菸死亡，而且這個數字還在不斷上升。健康專家說,到 2020 年,因吸菸而死亡的人數將達到一千萬,這個數字是很嚇人的。

在很多發達國家戒菸的人越來越多,相反在發展中國家吸菸的人越來越多。吸菸的陋習已傳到大、中學生裡去,甚至於有的小學生也吸起菸來。最小的菸民只有 8 ~ 10 歲。越來越多的年輕人吸菸是有多種原因的。其中最重要的一條就是,吸菸被認為是帥的表現,是一種時尚。最新研究證明,菸捲中有 5068 種不同種類的化合物,其中 69 種能致癌。吸菸可以引起 40 多種疾病,對孕婦來說更危險,因為吸菸會影響胎兒的健康,即化合物可進入胎兒的身體內,常常會造成新生兒畸形。

因此,世界衛生組織建議吸菸的人戒菸或減少吸菸量。

Lesson 20   Categories of Education in the United States

Education in the United States is usually divided into four levels. These are early childhood, elementary, secondary, and higher education. School attendance is required in every state of the United States. In most states, students must attend school until the age of sixteen.

The first level is early childhood education. This is for children under six years. Its main purpose is to prepare children for school. Children in kindergarten and preschool learn to get along in a group. They express their ideas and feelings by painting, singing, and playing. They are prepared for the learning experiences in elementary school.

The second level, elementary education, is for children from age six to twelve or fourteen. Elementary education is divided into six or eight grades. Children usually meet with one teacher for most of the day. They learn reading, arithmetic, writing, social studies, and science. They also have art, music, and physical education. They study various subjects and learn skills which prepare them for secondary education.

The third level is secondary education. It is for junior and senior high school students. Junior high school is usually for students from age twelve to fourteen. High school students are fourteen to seventeen or eighteen years old. Most American high schools have comprehensive programs. This means that a variety of subj ects are taught in the same school. Some students take courses to prepare themselves for college. Other students take technical or vocational courses that prepare them for jobs.

Higher education continues the educational process after high school. There are many kinds of institutions of higher education. Technical institutes offer two-year programs in electronics, engineering, business, and other subjects. Community or junior colleges also offer two-year programs. Some of these programs are vocational. Others are academic. After two years at a junior college, students receive an Associate degree. They can then continue at a four-year college. Many students go directly from high school to a four-year college or university. Colleges and universities offer many courses and programs. These lead to a Bachelor of Arts or a Bachelor of Science degree. Most universities also have professional schools. These provide training in business, education, engineering, law, and medicine.

(372 words)

 Vocabulary

1. category	n. 種類	
2. childhood	n. 孩童時期	
3. secondary	adj. 次要的，二級的，中級的，第二的	
4. attendance	n. 出席，出席的人數	
5. kindergarten	n. 幼兒園	
6. preschool	n. 幼兒園	
7. arithmetic	n. 算術，算法	
8. physical	adj. 身體的，物質的，自然的，物理的	
9. junior	adj. 年少的，下級的，後進的	
10.comprehensive	adj. 全面的，廣泛的	

11. vocational   adj. 職業的

12. graduate   n.（大學）畢業生，研究生／v.（大學）畢業

13. educational   adj. 教育的，教育性的

14. institution   n. 公共機構，協會，制度

15. institute   n. 學會，學院，協會

16. engineering   n. 工程（學）

17. associate   adj. 副的

18. directly   adv. 直接地，立即

19. bachelor   n. 單身漢，文理學士

20. professional   adj. 專業的，職業的

21. a variety of   多種多樣的

Useful Phrases and Expressions

1. Education in the United States is usually divided into four levels.

2. School attendance is required.

3. Its main purpose is to prepare children for school.

4. learn to get along in a group

5. They express their ideas and feelings by painting, singing and playing.

6. They are prepared for the learning experiences in...

7. Children usually meet with one teacher for most of the day.

8. They learn various subjects and skills to prepare them for secondary education.

9. It is for junior and senior high school students.

10. comprehensive programs

11. take courses to prepare themselves for college

12. take technical or vocational courses that prepare them for jobs after they graduate from high school

13. offer two-year program in electronics

14. community or junior colleges

15. Associate degree

16. These lead to a Bachelor of Arts or Bachelor of Science degree.

Exercises

I .Questions for Comprehension

1. How many levels does education in the United States have? What are they?

2. How old are children at the first level?

3. What do they learn at this level?

4. What is the purpose of the first level?

5. How old are children who go to the second level?

6. How many grades are there in elementary schools?

7. What do the students learn at the elementary schools?

8. How is secondary education divided?

9. What can this level of education offer to the students?

10. What do the students do after they graduate from high school?

11. What kinds of degrees can students get?

II.Essay Writing

　　Write an essay by putting together the answers to the questions in Exercise I, using such joining words as because, and, but and so on.

III.Questions for Discussion

1. Tell Chinese education system.

2. Make some comments on both the education system of the United States and our country.

IV.Translation

　　Put the following Chinese into English, using as many as possible the phrases and expressions you have learned.

1. 學好一門語言需要吃苦和進行大量的練習。

2. 開設這門課程主要是為了提供更多的機會來使用學過的語言知識。

3. 這個社區經常為居民舉辦各種各樣的活動，其中不少活動是專為退休人員舉辦的。

4. 德國政府為失業人員提供各種培訓，而這些培訓是免費的。所有的培訓課程都是實用性的（vocational），經過培訓後，失業人員可以再就業。

5. 通常一些人對自己的飲食習慣（eating habit）不是很注意，因為他們不知道不好的飲食習慣會導致各種各樣的疾病，如癌症、高血壓（high blood pressure）等。

Lesson 21　Cars That People Throw Away

A look at the roadsides of America, where ugly junked automobiles ruin the view from New York to California, makes one wonder whether any number of shredders can do all the work there is to do. In Philadelphia, the number of cars abandoned on the streets in a single year was over twenty-two thousand. In New York, it was eightytwo thousand. In San Francisco, police officer Thomas Hull says: "We're taking a hundred and twenty-five to a hundred and fifty abandoned cars off the streets every week, but people are leaving them faster than we can pick them up."

A number of reasons are given for the problem of people who just get out of their cars and walk away from them. First, there is the large number of used cars for sale, which makes it possible for a person to buy one for very little money and throw it away when something goes wrong. Second ’ there is the low trade-in value of old cars. And, of course, there is the increasing expense of having a car.

In spite of the difficulties, some cities and states are beginning to make progress. New York has taken many more abandoned cars off the streets in the last few years under a plan that puts the Sanitation Department in charge of this work. In Baltimore, city officials say they have cleared away most of the ownerless cars in the city by selling them to metal-shredding companies, and a similar program is under way in Chicago. In California, the state government has passed a new law under which all auto owners will pay one dollar extra, for one year only, to pay for one-time cleanup of cars that people throw away. There too the cars will be fed into machines.

Still, many difficulties remain, especially outside the cities. The cost of moving junked cars—even when they have been flattened to save space—is so high that it simply is not worthwhile to move a car if the shredding machine is more than two hundred miles away.

The first car shredder was built by Mr.Proler and his three brothers in 1958. Before that, they used a compression system that turns a car into a small square of metal in a few seconds. "The trouble is," says Mr.Proler, "that when you press the cars into a package, you have to press a lot of other stuff with it, and the result is poor quality steel when you melt it down. We wanted to get the high quality steel the car was made from and get rid of the glass, cloth, and other material. The new shredders do that for us."

With steel prices going up and many cities and states starting cleanup plans, the question of what to do with cars that people throw away may soon be answered. We will use the metal from junked cars to build new ones.

(488 words)

Vocabulary

1. shredder	n. 切菜器，粉碎機	
2. abandon	vt. 放棄，遺棄	
3. expense	n. 費用，代價，開支	
4. sanitation	n. 衛生，衛生設施	
5. ownerless	adj. 無主的	
6. shred	v. 撕碎，切碎	
7. cleanup	n. 清除，獲利	
8. flatten	vt. 使平，變平，打倒	
9. worthwhile	adj. 值得做的，值得出力的	

10. compression   n. 濃縮，壓縮，壓榨

11. stuff   n. 原料，材料，素材資料

12. melt   v.（使）融化，（使）熔化，使軟化

13. in spite of   不顧，不管

14. in charge of   負責；經營，管理

15. get rid of   擺脫，除掉

 ## Useful Phrases and Expressions

1. A look at... makes one wonder whether (why, when...)

2. ruin the view

3. take abandoned cars off streets

4. People are leaving them faster than we can pick them up.

5. A number of reasons are given for the problem.

6. walk away from

7. buy a car for very little money

8. There is the low trade-in value of old cars.

9. There is the increasing expense of having a car.

10. in spite of the difficulties

11. Sanitation Department

12. clean away most of the ownerless cars

13. A similar program is under way in Chicago.

14. Still many difficulties remain.

15. It simply is not worthwhile to move a car.

 **Exercises**

I .Comprehension Questions

1. What can people see at the roadsides from New York to California?

2. How serious is the problem of abandoned cars?

3. What causes this problem?

4. Has the government done anything?

5. Can the local governments solve the problem completely?

6. What did people do to abandoned cars before car shredders were invented?

7. What was the problem of this method of treating abandoned cars?

8. Why is it that the car shredders are better than compression system?

II .Essay Writing

Write an essay by putting together the answers to the questions in Exercise I, using such joining words as because, and, but and so on.

III .Questions for Discussion

1. Do you think China will also have the same problem of old cars? What shall we do?

2. Can you think of some other problems similar to those abandoned cars?

IV .Translation

Put the following Chinese into English, using as many as possible the phrases and expressions you have learned.

1. SARS 的出現使人們開始反思我們的醫療制度是否應當改進。

2. 有一件事一直使我感到不安。有一次，在大街上見到一個小偷在偷一位老人的錢，當時很多人都看見了，但誰都沒有採取任何行動。有的人走開了，有的站在那裡看著不說話，等小偷偷到錢走掉後才告訴老人他的錢被偷了。當時我也在場，可是我沒有勇氣出來抓這個小偷。我太自私了。

3. 國人為什麼有那麼多陋習，專家分析後歸納了幾大原因。

4. 昨天我們去外文書店花了近 3000 元買了 20 本特價書。

5. 我們系上有 20 臺電腦，已用了五年了。賣掉了不值錢，而這些電腦還是能用的。有人建議把這些電腦送給貧困地區的學校，有些人認為這樣做不好。儘管分歧很大，最後系裡還是決定把這些電腦送給偏鄉的一所小學。

Lesson 22   Aquaculture : New Hope for Food

Aquaculture or sea farming, as it is sometimes called—is one of the brightest hopes for finding an answer to the problem of a world food shortage. Although it may be years before aquaculture yields really large quantities of food, it is already partially successful. One of its successes is the growing of oysters.

Oyster farming is a big new business on Cape Cod, where the first large crop of oysters was harvested last October. The waters there were famous for delicious oysters until the supply gave out about fifteen years ago. "There's a whole generation of people who have never eaten oysters," says Karl Touraine, marketing director of Aqua Dynamics Corporation, a company that grows oysters on strings hanging from metal racks. "For about twenty years the oyster has been in short supply, and our aim is to reverse this by using new, modern growing techniques," he explains.

"Wareham, on Cape Cod, is the first place in the United States where oysters are being grown on racks in the off-bottom method," says Hank McAvoy of the National Marine Fisheries Service in Gloucester. "But there's nothing new about off-bottom raising," Mr.McAvoy adds. "It's been done successfully in Norway and Australia and, in the last few years, in Spain. The Japanese have used this form of aquaculture for years, and they're the most successful, with a yearly crop of forty-six thousand pounds of shelled oyster to the acre."

The Aqua Dynamics group grows oysters on strings, away from the bottom so that the oysters' natural enemies cannot reach them. "When an oyster can avoid enemies and live in unpolluted water with plenty to eat, he'll grow nice and fat in four years," Karl Touraine explains. "Oysters will fasten themselves onto almost anything they can," he continues. "At Wareham, we use shells, which we thread onto nylon strings hanging from metal racks. We lower the strings into the water, leaving at least a foot of water between the lowest shell and the bottom.

"So far the growth has been excellent and the taste j ust delightful," Mr.Touraine notes happily.

(354 words)

Vocabulary

1. shortage — n. 不足，缺乏
2. aquaculture — n. 水產業
3. yield — v. 出產，生長，生產 ／ n. 產量，收益
4. partially — adv. 部分地
5. oyster — n. <動> 牡蠣，蠔
6. cape — n. 海角，岬
7. dynamics — n. 動力學
8. corporation — n. <律> 公司，企業，（美）有限公司
9. string — n. 線，細繩，一串，一行
10. rack — n. 架，行李架
11. reverse — vt. 顛倒，倒轉
12. marine — n. 海運業 ／ adj. 海的，海產的，航海的，海運的
13. fishery — n. 漁業，水產業，漁場
14. Spain — n. 西班牙（歐洲南部國家）
15. yearly — adj. 每年的
16. shell — n. 貝殼，殼，外形，砲彈

17. acre	n. 英畝
18. unpolluted	adj. 未受汙染的，清潔的
19. fasten	vt. 扎牢，扣住，拴緊，使固定
20. nylon	n. 尼龍
21. delightful	adj. 令人愉快的，可喜的

 Useful Phrases and Expressions

1. the brightest hopes for finding an answer to the problem of a world food shortage

2. It may be years before...

3. It is already partially successful.

4. One of its successes is...

5. The supply gave out about...

6. grow oyster

7. The oyster has been in short supply.

8. Our aim is to reverse...

9. modern growing techniques

10. There is nothing new about...

11. It's been done successfully in...

12. The taste is just delightful...

 Exercises

Ⅰ.Comprehension Questions

1. Why do people take a new interest in aquaculture?

2. Was this idea already proved?

3. For how long has the oyster been in short supply?

4. What has been done to reverse this short supply?

5. What is the result?

6. How is the quality of the oysters?

7. Why is this off-bottom method good?

II .Essay Writing

Write an essay by putting together the answers to the questions in Exercise I, using such joining words as because, and, but and so on.

III .Questions for Discussion

1. What do you think of this idea of using aquaculture to solve the problem of a world food shortage?

2. Is this idea helpful to our country?

IV .Translation

Put the following Chinese into English, using as many as possible the phrases and expressions you have learned.

1. 酒精 (alcohol) 作為飛機燃料在巴西 (Brazil) 已試驗成功。巴西為解決世界能源短缺問題找到了一個出路。用酒精做燃料的最大優勢 (advantage) 是價格便宜,無汙染。它的供應永遠不會枯竭。幾乎每個國家都能很容易地製造酒精。

2. 老鼠的天敵是貓。人們就會問,為什麼貓要吃老鼠呢?科學家發現,貓為了晚上能看見東西需要一種物質 (substance) ,而這種物質只有老鼠體內有。

3. 很多專家擔心汽油的供應將會比停車位快。現在在市中心已很難找到停車
   的地方。不出幾年，人們就會發現馬路上全是汽車，車速比走路還慢。到
   那時候汽車還有什麼用？

Lesson 23   Carry on a Proud Tradition

I met him first on a summer day in 1986. I had rushed into his ugly little shop to have the heels of my shoes repaired. It wasn't much of a job, so I waited while he did it. He greeted me with a cheerful smile. "You're new in this neighborhood, aren't you?"

I said that I was. I had moved into a house at the end of the street only a week before.

"This is a fine neighborhood," he said. "You'll be happy here."

I sat there with my shoes off, watching as he got ready to make the repairs. Sadly he looked at the leather covering the heel. It was worn through because I had failed to have the repair job done a month ago. I grew a little impatient, for I was rushing to meet a friend. "Please hurry," I begged.

He looked at me over his spectacles. "Now, lady, we won't be long, I want to do a good job." He was silent for a moment. "You see, I have a tradition to live up to."

A tradition? In this ugly little shop that was not different from so many other shoe-repair shops on the side streets of New York?

He must have felt my surprise, for he smiled as he went on. "Yes, lady, I inherited a tradition. My father and my grandfather were shoemakers, and they were the best. My father always told me, 'Son, do the best job on every shoe that comes into the shop, and be proud of your fine work. Do that always, and you'll have both happiness and money enough to live on.'"

As he handed me the finished shoes, he said, "These will last a long time. I've used good leather."

I left in a hurry because I was late and my friend would be waiting for me impatiently. But I had a warm and grateful feeling. On my way home I passed the little shop again. There he was, still working. He saw me, and to my surprise he waved and smiled. This was the beginning of our friendship. It was a friendship that came to mean more and more to me as the time passed.

Every day as I passed his shop, we waved to each other in friendly greeting. At first I went in only when I had repair work to be done. Then I found myself going in every few days just to talk with him.

He was a tall man, but bent from long years of work. His hair was gray and there wasn't much of it. His face was deeply lined. But I remember best his fine dark eyes, alive with kindness and humor.

One day I came away from my house disappointed and angry because of a poor job some painters had done for me. My friend waved to me as I went by, so I went into his shop for comfort. He let me go on talking angrily about the poor work and carelessness of presentday workmen. "They had no pride in their work," I said. "They didn't want to work. They just wanted to collect their money for doing nothing."

He agreed. "There's a lot of that kind around, but maybe we should not blame them. Maybe their fathers had no pride in their work. That's hard on a boy. It keeps him from learning something that is important."

"What can be done about it?" I asked.

He waited a minute before answering, then looked at me seriously. "There is only one way. Every man or woman who hasn't inherited a proud tradition must start building one."

"In this country, our freedom lets each of us make his own contribution. We must make it a good contribution. No matter what sort of work a man does, if he gives it his best each day, he's start ing a tradition for his children to live up to. And he is making lots of happiness for himself," added he.

On the way home I thought his words over and over.

(678 words)

 Vocabulary

1.	proud	adj. 自豪的，感到光榮的
2.	tradition	n. 傳統，慣例
3.	heel	n. 腳後跟，踵，跟部
4.	cheerful	adj. 愉快的，高興的
5.	leather	n. 皮革，皮革製品
6.	impatient	adj. 不耐煩的，不耐心的
7.	spectacle	n. 眼鏡
8.	inherit	vt. 繼承，遺傳而得
9.	shoemaker	n. 皮鞋匠
10.	impatiently	adv. 無耐性地
11.	grateful	adj. 感激的，感謝的
12.	humor	n. 幽默，詼諧
13.	painter	n. 畫家，油漆匠
14.	workman	n. 工人，工匠
15.	contribution	n. 捐獻，貢獻

Useful Phrases and Expressions

1. It wasn't much of a job.

2. He greeted me with a cheerful smile.

3. at the end of the street

4. This is a fine neighborhood.

5. make the repairs

6. It was worn through.

7. I was rushing to meet a friend.

8. We won't be long.

9. I have a tradition to live up to.

10. side streets

11. I inherited a tradition.

12. be proud of your fine work

13. finished shoes

14. These will last for a long time.

15. I had a warm and grateful feeling.

16. He was bent from long years of work.

17. His face was deeply lined.

18. I remembered best his fine dark eyes.

19. I went into his shop for comfort.

20. present-day workmen.

21. They had no pride in their work.

22. They didn't want to work. They just wanted to collect their money for doing nothing.

23. That's hard on a boy.

24. There's a lot of that kind around.

25. It keeps him from learning something that is important.

26. There is only one way.

27. He gives it his best each day.

 Exercises

I .Comprehension Questions

1. What did the writer do on a summer day in 1986?

2. What did the shoe repairer do about her shoes?

3. Why did she grow impatient?

4. What did he tell the writer?

5. What did the shoe repairer's father and grandfather do?

6. What did his father always tell him?

7. When he finished the shoes, what did he say to the writer?

8. What happened from then on?

9. What were the facts to show that they became friends?

10. Why did the writer visit him one day?

11. Did he listen to her?

12. What did he say after she finished her story?

13. What did the shoe repairer think should be done?

II .Essay Writing

Write an essay by putting together the answers to the questions in Exercise I, using such joining words as because, and, but and so on.

III .Questions for Discussion

1. Do you think the shoe repairer was old-fashioned? What are your arguments?

2. Does the story look like a true story? Why?

3. How was it possible that the writer and the shoe repairer could become friends?

IV .Translation

Put the following Chinese into English, using as many as possible the phrases and expressions you have learned.

五年前康凱從高雄一所技職院校專科部畢業，他的大部分朋友都選擇繼續升學，但他不想再唸書了，他想先工作。他的父母親都支持他的想法，因為他們認為，先累積一點工作經驗對他有好處，到那時他會清楚自己要幹什麼。康凱的父母都是平凡的農民，種稻子的。他們對兒子寄予了很大的厚望。

康凱參加了很多面試，但人家都要求學士或碩士學位的人，康凱只有專科文憑，因此對他來說要找一份工作不那麼容易。他有些不耐煩了，想放棄找工作的念頭。然而有一天，他的老師幫他在一家貿易公司找了一份工作，那家公司不算太大，但生意很好，人際關係也很好。總經理是一位中年女士，很和善但也很嚴格。她跟手下人說話總是帶著微笑，她讓康凱先在收發室工作，任務是收發信件和報刊雜誌。起初他很失望，因為他覺得這算不上什麼工作。但工作了 10 天後，他發現他的工作沒有他想像得那麼容易。在這 10 天裡，他犯了三次錯誤。有一次他沒能將一份很重要的包裹寄出，差一點造成 50 萬元的財務損失。從此，他開始認真地對待他的工作，並決心將工作做好。在接下來的兩年裡，他成了一名從不犯錯誤的員工，並被調到另外一個部門去做一份新的有挑戰性的工作。

Lesson 24　Alternative Medicine— Acupuncture

People who are used to taking drugs or medicines when they are ill, or who expect to have an operation in a hospital, find the idea of acupuncture very strange. In fact, acupuncture is a much older form of medicine than allopathy, which is what most doctors practice in the West. It began in ancient China, and although it seems to be unscientific to Western minds, its principles are precise, and based on a belief that man is a spiritual creature, as well as a physical one.

According to acupuncture, the human body contains twelve invisible pathways, or lines, which pass through it. These pathways are called meridians, and they are quite different from the physical nervous system well-known to Western doctors. These meridians carry a life force, which must be able to flow easily through the body. If it can't, their body becomes ill.

The skilled acupuncturist learns where the meridians are, and how each one influences different parts of the body and the mind. To treat a patient, he puts a needle made of stainless steel into the skin at an exact place on the meridian. Normally, the patient feels no pain. The needle starts a current, which travels through the meridian to the physical nervous system. The part of the body which is ill then responds to the impulse carried on the current. The acupuncturist inserts the needles in different places and turns them clockwise or anti-clockwise according to the effect he wants to produce. This can mean that a needle is inserted into the back of the knee to treat headaches, for example. To an acupuncturist, the parts of the body work together in a way that Western medicine cannot understand.

Behind the healing power of acupuncture are the ancient Chinese ideas of Yin and Yang—two forces which both oppose and complement each other. It is difficult for Westerners to understand Yin and Yang, but we can think of complementary opposites such as male and female, night and day, positive and negative electrical charges, birth and death. To the Chinese, everything in the world is either Yin or Yang, and the balance of the two forces is essential for peace and harmony. Disease and illness of the body occur when the balance of Yin and Yang in it is upset. Acupuncture can help to restore this balance.

What can this form of medicine cure? Its followers say it can treat many illnesses, including stomach disorders, spinal diseases and headaches. It can be used as an anaesthetic, and in one hospital in Britain, women giving birth are offered acupuncture instead of pain-killing drugs. However, the most important aspect of acupuncture for Westerners is that it can help where allopathy has failed.

(457 words)

 Vocabulary

1.	alternative	adj. 選擇性的，兩者擇一的
2.	acupuncture	n. 針灸療法
3.	acupuncturist	n. 針灸醫生
4.	allopathy	n. ＜醫＞對抗療法
5.	practice	n. 實行，實踐
6.	principle	n. 法則，原則，原理
7.	precise	adj. 精確的，準確的
8.	creature	n. 人，動物

9. invisible   adj. 看不見的，無形的

10. pathway   n. 路，徑

11. meridian   n. 子午線，正午

12. current   n. 氣流，電流，水流

13. insert   vt. 插入，嵌入

14. heal   v. 治癒，醫治，結束

15. oppose   v. 反對，使對立，使對抗，抗爭

16. complement   vt. 補助，補足

17. complementary adj. 補充的，補足的

18. charge   n. 負荷，電荷

19. essential   adj. 本質的，實質的，基本的

20. peace   n. 和平，和睦，安寧，靜寂

21. harmony   n. 協調，融洽

22. restore   vt. 恢復，使回覆

23. follower   n. 追隨者，信徒

24. spinal   adj. 脊骨的，脊髓的

25. anaesthetic   n. 麻醉劑

26. aspect   n.（問題等的）方面

 ## Useful Phrases and Expressions

1. find the idea of acupuncture very strange

2. a much older form of medicine

3. Its principles are precise.

4. be based on a belief that...

5. nervous system

6. respond to

7. according to the effect he wants to produce

8. This can mean that...

9. The parts of the body work together in a way that...

10. Both oppose and complement each other.

11. 1 complementary opposites

12. The balance of Yin and Yang is upset.

13. 1 restore this balance

14. The most important aspect of acupuncture is that...

 Exercises

I .Comprehension Questions

1. What is acupuncture?

2. How do the Western people find it? Why?

3. Are its principles precise? What are they based on?

4. Explain the belief.

5. What do the skilled acupuncturist learn?

6. How does he treat a patient?

7. What do the Chinese think of everything in the world?

8. Why does the body become ill?

9. How can the acupuncture help?

10. How good is acupuncture?

II.Essay Writing

Write an essay by putting together the answers to the questions in Exercise I, using such joining words as because, and, but and so on.

III.Questions for Discussion

1. Why can acupuncture work as an alternative medicine? Do you believe acupuncture? Why?

2. What do you think of its future? Why?

3. Do you believe that acupuncture is unscientific? Why?

4. What advantages does acupuncture have?

IV.Translation

Put the following Chinese into English, using as many as possible the phrases and expressions you have learned.

馬克·漢生（Mark Hansen）曾經是一位十分出色的超市經理，他在紐約最大的連鎖超市中的一家店工作了 20 年，事業十分成功。然而，三年前他中風，有一段時間甚至出現了病危。醫生想盡了一切辦法來挽救他的生命，可是所用的藥都不起作用。醫生告訴他的妻子，馬克很可能只有幾星期可活。可是他的妻子瑪莎不願放棄可以挽救馬克的其他辦法。她告訴醫生她認識在唐人街的一位中醫，他在紐約的中國人裡很有名氣，治好了很多西醫看不好的病人。她的一個好朋友就是其中之一，她曾患有脊椎病，走路很困難，是這位中醫把她的病治好了。他在她的腳心、腿和背上扎了好幾針。經過一個月的治療，她走路不費力了，完全可以像正常人一樣走路。因此，瑪莎建議醫院請這位中醫來會診。剛開始醫院不同意她的意見，他們認為中醫不科學。可是瑪莎堅持她的意見，最後醫院同意了。這位中醫對馬克用了中藥和針灸療法。三個療程後，馬克不但脫離了生命危險，而且還可以起來散步了。針灸治療繼續進行了兩個月，等治療結束時，馬克完全恢復了。從此以後，他和瑪莎就對中醫堅信不移。

Lesson 25   Cheaper and Better than Drugs

Herbalism is a way of helping the body to build up its natural defenses to illness by using plants or herbs. People who practice natural medicine believe that the body contains repairing processes within itself. Natural substances can activate these processes. Homeopaths believe that what harms when taken in quantity can heal when a little is taken to build up the body's resistance. So the principle of homeopathy is the opposite of the principle of much current Western medicine, allopathy. Allopathy uses substances which are quite different from the substances in the body which are causing harm.

Herbalists point out the dangers of using modern drugs, which often have harmful side-effects. By using herbs, they say, a cure can be achieved which does more than just treat individual symptoms. Extracts from herbs, if they are used for a long time can heal the whole organism rather than just temporarily treat a disturbance in the body. So using natural remedies is more effective in the end, as well as being safer and cheaper as a method. Indeed, the World Health Organization looked at traditional medicine, and particularly herbal remedies, in 1977, and concluded that using local resources of medicinal herbs would be effective. They said that herbs do often cure, and that using them would reduce the drug bill of many developing countries.

Herbs are prepared in many different ways. The most common way is to make an infusion. You pour water over the herb and boil it for half an hour or forty minutes and boil twice. A decoction is when you simmer the herb with water over a low fire until a third of the water has steamed away. Then you divide the liquid into two equal portions, one for the morning and the other for the evening. You make ointments by cooking animal fat with the herb and leaving it to set; poultices are hot applications of the herb itself to the inflamed areas of the skin. Herbs to cure insomnia are stuffed into pillows. Different herbs cure different diseases.

(342 words)

 Vocabulary

1. herbalism	n. 草藥學	
2. herb	n. 藥草，香草	
3. herbalist	n. 藥草採集者；草本植物學家	
4. defense	n. 防衛，防衛物	
5. substance	n. 物質，實質	
6. resistance	n. 抵抗力，反抗，抵抗	
7. side effect	副作用	
8. individual	n. 個人，個體／adj. 個別的，單獨的，個人的	
9. symptom	n. <醫><植>症狀，徵兆	
10. extract	n. 精，汁，榨出物；摘錄	
11. organism	n. 生物體，有機體	
12. temporarily	adv. 臨時地	
13. disturbance	n. 騷動，打擾，干擾	
14. remedy	n. 藥物，治療法	
15. particularly	adv. 獨特地，顯著地	
16. infusion	n. 浸液，浸（泡）劑	
17. decoction	n. 煎煮，煎熬的藥	

18. simmer   vt. 慢煮／vi. 煨，炖

19. liquid   n. 液體，流體

20. portion   n. 一部分，一份

21. ointment   n. 藥膏，油膏

22. poultice   n. 膏狀藥

23. application   n. 施用，敷用

24. inflame   vt. 使腫，使發炎

25. insomnia   n. 失眠，失眠症

26. stuff   vt. 塞滿，填滿，填充

27. pillow   n. 枕頭，枕墊

Useful Phrases and Expressions

1. build up the body's natural defenses (resistance) to illness

2. repairing processes

3. activate the processes

4. side-effect(s)

5. treat individual symptoms

6. heal the whole organism

7. temporarily treat a disturbance in the body

8. is more effective in the end

9. herbal remedies

10. reduce the drug bill

11. Herbs are prepared in many different ways.

12. Different herbs cure different diseases.

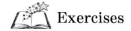 **Exercises**

I.Comprehension Questions

1. What is so good about herbalism?

2. What processes does our body contain?

3. How can natural medicine help our body?

4. What is the danger of using drugs according to herbalists?

5. What are the advantages of using herbal medicine?

6. What did WHO say about herbs in 1977?

7. How is herbal medicine prepared?

8. What is the most common way to prepare a decoction?

II.Essay Writing

Write an essay by putting together the answers to the questions in Exercise I, using such joining words as because, and, but and so on.

III.Questions for Discussion

1. Do you think herbal medicine has a bright future? Why do you think so?

2. Are there any disadvantages of herbal medicine? What are they, if there are any?

3. If one of your good friends has some disturbance in the body, what would you advise him or her to do?

IV.Translation

Put the following Chinese into English, using as many as possible the phrases and expressions you have learned.

1. 到一家大超市的食品部看一看，你會發現貨架上有成千上萬種食品。火腿、燻雞、燻鴨、午餐肉等熟食很受青睞，尤其是那些忙碌的人特別喜愛這些熟食。這些熟食不便宜，但買的人很多，原因是這些食品既方便，又好吃。然而現在有一種新的趨勢，即拒絕熟食，因為這些食品中含有的添加劑和防腐劑可能會致癌。現在越來越多的人意識到了這些化學品的危害，他們更喜歡新鮮的雞鴨肉。

2. 經過長期的研究，世界衛生組織得出一個結論：世界上最好的飲料是茶，特別是綠茶。茶之所以成為最佳飲料是因為它含有蛋白質、脂肪、維生素C、維生素 D、維生素 E 及多種礦物質。這些都是我們身體所必需的營養素。科學家發現茶中含有 300 多種天然物質，其中一些可以防癌並增強我們對疾病的抵抗力。茶葉中含有一種物質，它能防止一種有毒化學成分在我們體內形成，而這種化學成分可以致癌。在四川有一個很有趣的發現，一些山區的村莊裡沒有人得過癌症。衛生專家們經過大量的研究發現，出現這種情況的重要原因之一是那裡的村民世代都有喝茶的習慣。

Book Two

▌Lesson 1　Background Music

Advertising through pictures, words and images is a very obvious part of the world we live in today. On television and on the radio, in the streets, at the cinema and in newspapers and magazines, advertisements tell us to buy every kind of product. We are aware, though often not completely, of this kind of selling through words and pictures. But we often forget that music is one of the most powerful methods of selling things in the modern western world.

Music is, of course, a very important part of television, radio and cinema advertisements. But frequently it is used by itself, as a background to our daily lives in supermarkets, restaurants, hotels, banks, factories, department stores and airports when we are not aware of it. The dangerous thing about background music is that people are not conscious of it most of the time, and therefore do not realize that it is being used to sell products and to make them spend more money.

So how exactly is background music used to "help" us spend money? One example is the Hilton Hotel in London. There the music played in the rooms of the hotel is so soft, you hardly notice it. Ken Faulks, sales director of the company, which planned the music for the Hilton, says that its purpose is to relax people. "In an expensive hotel, the idea is to make the customers relax. The more time they spend sitting there, the more money they spend—and because they are so relaxed, they don't care." Background music can also be used for the opposite purpose, to make people leave a place. Bob Peyton, who owns the Chicago Pizza Pie Factory in London says,

"When people have finished eating at my restaurant, the kind of music we play makes them want to move off, so they leave quickly!"

Background music isn't only used in places like hotels and restaurants. It is also used for people at work in companies and factories. The head of an insurance company in London says, "We play music to people who are doing boring, routine jobs. We find that they work better and the music makes them more cheerful."

In America, a very effective method of advertising through music is being used. Words are spoken very softly as the music is played, Dr. Hal Becker of a company called Audio Visual Techniques Corporation describes how their special tapes are used in shops. Six large American department stores played tapes with music and a voice telling shoppers not to shoplift. Surprisingly, 33% less goods were stolen from the stores.

This technique is called "subliminal" advertising. It works by telling people to do things without them knowing this is happening. In the store people don't notice the voice, but unconsciously they do what they are told to do. Perhaps this is a good use of technique, but how long will it be before the instruction "Do not steal" is changed to"Buy product X"?

When you go out today, notice where and when you hear music being played. Is it there just to make you feel cheerful, or does it have a more serious commercial purpose to make you spend money without knowing quite why you are doing it?

(544 words)

 Useful Phrases and Expressions

1. advertising through pictures and words

2. ...is a very obvious part of the world we live in.

3. be aware of/be aware that

4. one of the most powerful methods of selling things

5. The dangerous thing about background music is that...

6. People are not conscious of it.

7. It is being used to sell...

8. You hardly notice it.

9. Its purpose is to...

10. an expensive hotel

11. use for the opposite purpose

12. make them want to move off

13. people at work

14. do boring and routine jobs

15. a very effective method of

16. shoplift

17. It works by telling people...

18. without knowing that this is happening

19. This is a good use of the technique.

20. How long will it be before...?

 ## Exercises

I .Comprehension Questions

1. What role does music play in television, radio and cinema advertisement?

2. Where else music is also used? As what?

3. What is the purpose of background music? Give an example.

4. Can background music be used for opposite purpose? What is the opposite purpose? Can you give one example?

5. Why is music played in companies and factories?

6. According to the passage, how is music used in big department stores in America?

7. What is this technique called?

8. How does it work?

II .Essay Writing

Write an essay by putting together the answers to the questions in Exercise I, using such joining words as because, and, but and so on.

III .Questions for Discussion

1. Do you agree that background music is a very powerful method of selling things? Give some good examples to show your views.

2. Find out what other places where background music is used for a special purpose.

IV .Translation

Put the following Chinese into English, using as many as possible the phrases and expressions you have learned.

1. 世界上第一輛自行車是一個法國人在 1790 年發明的。它非常簡單，沒有鏈子、腳蹬和車把。騎車人用腳蹬地讓車走，又慢又不舒服。人們花了差不多一個世紀才把自行車改進成今天的樣子。1888 年，一個英國人製造出第一輛現代自行車。從此以後，自行車就成為了人們生活中的一部分。1960 年代，西方把中國稱為自行車王國。無論在城市還是在農村，自行車是主要的交通工具，在城市裡上下班時間馬路上全是自行車。但這已經成為歷史了。現在自行車漸漸被小汽車代替了。城市裡的空氣越來越不好，不知要隔多久中國才能再次成為自行車王國。

2. 你去一個城市或國家出差，想和家人或朋友聯繫，什麼方式最快、最容易、最便宜？你會不加思索地說手機。手機確實使生活方便多了，你可以在任何時間、地點和家人或朋友聯繫。如果你不想跟他們說話，可以發簡訊。智慧型手機還可以拍照。然而需要警覺的是，手機有害於大腦。一般人們不會感覺到這種危害，因為這種危害過程很慢。健康專家提醒說，為防止手機對大腦的傷害，最好的辦法是不要長時間用它，特別是在開車時不要用。

Lesson 2   Rubbish Need Not Be Wasted

China could start building incinerator plants which burn household garbage and other trash. Excluded would be industrial waste. These plants would operate in the following manner.

Garbage trucks would dump the refuse into a large chamber. "Spotters, "people who supervise the dumping process, would then call in bulldozers to push aside harmful objects. These may be such things as industrial waste containers or items that would damage the machinery. Almost anything else in the form of household garbage can be processed.

Above, in glass-enclosed offices, are operators who control giant claws. These claws pick up three tons of garbage and drop it into chutes that go to the furnaces. A small window allows the viewer to observe the silently-ranging fire. Moving grates stir the material to guarantee complete burning. These fires heat boilers which produce steam. Steam drives turbines which generate electricity.

Do these plants emit smoke containing harmful pollutants? No, when properly managed, these plants do not contaminate or pollute the atmosphere. Traditionally there has been a fear that hazardous dioxins would come out of the smokestacks of these incinerators. Dioxins are a group of 75 chemical compounds, two of which are said to cause cancer. Scientists at the United States Environmental Protection Agency have shown the dioxins breakdown when burned at 1600 degrees Fahrenheit. The temperature in the furnace is 2800 degrees Fahrenheit. This is more than hot enough to eliminate toxic emissions.

Where are some of these plants currently operating? The Kingdom of Monaco has one. On its roof are public tennis courts and inside is a pleasant restaurant. The plant is within 500 yards of Prince Rainier's Palace. There are approximately 350 plants spread through Brazil, Russia, Japan, and Western Europe.

It is estimated that this mass-burning technology will continue to grow. Countries are seeking efficient means of disposing of everincreasing amounts of garbage.

In America incinerator plants have been successfully operating since the early 1970s in States such as Massachusetts, California, Florida, New York and Maryland.

(332 words)

Useful Phrases and Expressions

1. household garbage

2. Excluded would be industrial waste.

3. These plants would operate in the following manner.

4. call in bulldozers to push aside harmful objects

5. such things as

6. Almost anything else in the form of... can be processed.

7. in glass-enclosed offices

8. A small window allows the viewer to observe...

9. Plants emit smoke containing harmful pollutants.

10. when properly managed

11. Traditionally there has been a fear that...

12. two of which are said to cause cancer

13. This is more than (+ adj.) enough to do somrthing

14. a pleasant restaurant

15. There are approximately 350 plants spread through...

16. it is estimated that...

17. sth. will continue to grow

18. ever-increasing

 Exercises

I .Comprehension Questions

1. What does the writer think China could do? Why?

2. How is it that garbage can be used to generate electricity?

3. What are the things that people are worried about?

4. Will these things happen? Why?

5. What have the scientists at United States Environmental Protection Agency shown?

6. Is this temperature hot enough to eliminate emissions?

7. Where can we find these incinerator plants?

8. Will this mass-burning technology continue to grow? Why?

II .Essay Writing

Write an essay by putting together the answers to the questions in Exercise I, using such joining words as because, and, but and so on.

III .Questions for Discussion

1. Is garbage a serious problem in our country? Why do you think so? Is it possible to solve this problem? How?

2. Why is it that the amount of household garbage is increasing all the time in our country? Do you think it is necessary to ask people to reduce the amount of household garbage they produce?

IV .Translation

Put the following Chinese into English, using as many as possible the phrases and expressions you have learned.

1. 據報導，中國 16% 的人口是 60 歲以上的老人。其中 80 歲以上的老人約有 2000 萬。由於醫療條件的改善和生活水準的不斷提高，老齡人口不斷增加。估計到 2050 年中國大約有 5 億老年人。中國社會己開始步入老齡化，如果這個問題處理不當，將會引起很多社會問題。因此，中國政府應馬上著手建立一套合理的福利制度，以確保老年人能無憂無慮地度過晚年。

2. 日本是全世界最清潔的國家之一，馬路上見不到垃圾桶。在日本，在馬路上或其他公共場所亂扔廢棄物是違法的。孩子們從小就學會了如何處理垃圾。每晚人們把垃圾袋放在自家門口，夜間垃圾車收集後直接運往垃圾焚燒廠。從機場到東京的路上人們會見到一些像公園一樣的高煙囱工廠，工廠周圍種滿了鮮花和綠草坪，那些工廠是垃圾焚燒廠。東京的一部分用電來自於這裡。

Lesson 3 The Only Thing People Are Interested in Today Is Earning More Money

Once upon a time there lived a beautiful young woman and a handsome young man. They were very poor, but as they were deeply in love, they wanted to get married. The young people's parents shook their heads. "You can't get married yet," they said. "Wait till you get a good job with good prospects." So the young people waited until they found good jobs with good prospects and they were able to get married. They were still poor, of course. They didn't have a house to live in or have any furniture, but that didn't matter. The young man had a good job with good prospects, so large organizations lent him the money he needed to buy a house, some furniture, all the latest electrical appliances and a car. The couple lived happily, even after paying off debts, for the rest of their lives. And so ends another modern romantic fable.

We live in a materialistic society and are trained from our earliest years to be acquisitive. Our possessions, "mine" and "yours" are clearly labelled from early childhood. When we grow old enough to earn a living, it does not surprise us to discover that success is measured in terms of the money you earn. We spend the whole of our lives keeping up with our neighbours, the Joneses. If we buy a new television set, Jones is bound to buy a bigger and better one. If we buy a new car, we can be sure that the Joneses will go and get two new cars: one for his wife and one for himself. The most amusing thing about this game is that the Joneses and all the neighbours who are struggling frantically to keep up with them are spending borrowed money kindly provided, at a suitable rate of interest, of course by friendly banks, insurance companies, etc.

It is not only in affluent societies that people are obsessed with ideas of making more money. Consumer goods are desirable everywhere and modern industry deliberately sets out to create new markets. Gone are the days when industrial goods were made to last forever. The wheels of industry must be kept turning. "Built-in obsolescence" provides the means: goods are made to be discarded. Cars get tinier and tinier. You no sooner acquire this year's model than you are thinking about its replacement.

This materialistic outlook has seriously influenced education. Fewer and fewer young people these days acquire knowledge only for its own sake. Every course of studies must lead somewhere: i.e.to a bigger wage packet. The demand for skilled personnel far exceeds the supply and big companies compete with each other to recruit students before they have completed their studies. Tempting salaries and fringe benefits are offered to them. Recruiting tactics of this kind have led to the "brain drain". Highly skilled people offer their services to the highest bidder. The wealthier nations deprive their poorer neighbours of their most able citizens. While money is worshipped as ever before, the rich get richer and the poor, poorer.

(518 words)

 Useful Phrases and Expressions

1. a good job with prospects

2. electrical appliances

3. pay off debts

4. live in a materialistic society

5. be trained from one's earliest years to be acquisitive

6. It doesn't surprise us to discover that...

7. Success is measured in terms of the money you earn.

8. We spend the whole of our lives keeping up with our neighbours.

9. be bound to...

10. We can be sure that...

11. The most amusing thing about... is that...

12. affluent societies

13. People are obsessed with ideas of making more money.

14. Consumer goods are desirable.

15. Modern industry deliberately sets out to create new markets.

16. built-in obsolescence

17. Goods are made to be discarded.

18. Materialistic outlook has seriously influenced education.

19. The demand for... far exceeds the supply.

20. tempting salaries and fringe benefit

21. brain drain

22. able citizens

23. Money is worshipped.

 Exercises

I .Comprehension Questions

1. What kind of society do we live in?

2. What do people think about all the time in this society? Why?

3. What are people trained from their earliest years?

4. How do they spend their whole lives?

5. What do you find about goods and modern industry in affluent societies?

6. Do the industrial goods last for a long time now? Why?

7. Has this materialistic outlook influenced anything?

8. Do young people learn knowledge for learning knowledge?

9. Is this a big demand for skilled people? Can this society meet the demand?

10. What is the result of this shortage?

11. How do the big companies compete with each other?

12. Why do the highly skilled people go to the highest bidder?

13. What do the wealthier nations do to the poor nations? What is the result?

II .Essay Writing

Write an essay by putting together the answers to the questions in Exercise I, using such joining words as because, and, but and so on.

III .Questions for Discussion

1. Everybody wants to be successful. How do your measure your success?

2. What is your outlook on money? Do you agree with the idea that the more money you have the happier you are? Why?

IV .Translation

Put the following Chinese into English, using as many as possible the phrases and expressions you have learned.

　　自從 1980 年代起，華人的金錢觀念在不斷地變化。華人向來有存錢的習慣，孩子從小就學會不亂花錢，經濟條件不允許的東西不要買。然而現在越來越多的人，尤其是有些青年人不再喜歡存錢了。他們的想法是：有錢就花，買不起的東西可以借錢買，今天可花明天的錢。說來這種想法也不足為怪。逐漸富裕了，物質產品越來越豐富，處處是誘人的商品讓你不得不買。但只要有一份好的工作、好的前景，你可以向銀行貸款買房子和汽車。銀行願意借錢給你因為他們可以收取利息，借錢的利率遠遠高於存錢的利率。如果你借 600 萬元買一套三房一廳的房子，等你還完債時你也許付了 680 萬，銀行賺了你 80 萬。而你為了還債拚命賺錢，賺得多花得也多。

Lesson 4　Millions of Oliver Twists Live in Streets

Whether runaways, school dropouts or abandoned children for whom the street is home can be numbered by the tens of million. "Their number seems to rise as countries become more and more urbanized, and big cities like Calcutta, Nairobi, Marseilles, New York and Bogota are monuments to their plight," according to a United Nations report just released.

In groups of three, five or ten, they often form closely knit families, feeling closer to street siblings than to their own brothers and sisters in their former homes, Peter Tacon, of the UN Children's Funds (UNICEF) told Reuters in an interview. Tacon, who deals with the organization's programs for street children, said youngsters of up to 19 years living a street life could be roughly estimated at 90 million in Third World nations, with another 10 million in industrial countries.

The problem seems greatest in South America. UNICEF quoted a report from Brazil that put the number of street children there as high as a staggering 30 million.

UNICEF included children working on the streets but who still had family ties and those who were living entirely cut off from home. "They often form groups which become so cohesive that they function like mobile mini-societies, providing members with a security and solidarity not experienced before," Tacon said. He cited the example of Rio de Janeiro, where street children are "everywhere, in the parks in gangs, in the boulevards as snack vendors, and every night under a piece of cardboard or plastic wrapping huddled asleep on the beaches".

A large majority are on the street to work and earn a little money to help support their families. But many are left to survive on their own with no protection after fleeing violence in slum homes or being kicked out or abandoned by adults no longer able to support them.

Tacon cited recession and migration to cities as the main reasons why South America was becoming "the spawning ground for the Oliver Twists of the 20thcentury"—a reference to the orphan children in Charles Dickens' 19th-century tale of urban poverty.

UNICEF has helped set up a number of programs, particularly in Brazil, whereby street educators try to combine schooling with part-time work. These include workshops in weaving, ceramic, leatherworks, and other crafts.

(392 words)

 Useful Phrases and Expressions

1. runaways, school dropouts, abandoned children

2. can be numbered by the tens of million

3. The number seems to rise.

4. Countries become more and more urbanized.

5. be monuments to

6. in groups of three, five or ten

7. closely-knit

8. Street children live a street life.

9. be roughly estimated

10. The problem seems greatest in...

11. have family ties

12. live entirely cut off from home

13. Many are left to survive on their own.

14. cite... as the main reasons why...

15. the spawning ground for

 Exercises

I .Comprehension Questions

1. According to a report by the United Nations, is there a huge number of street children in big cities? Give some names of the big cities.

2. Does the number keep rising? Why?

3. Who are these street children?

4. Why are they called street children?

5. Why do they form closely-knit families?

6. What do the maj ority do on the street?

7. Who is Peter Tacon?

8. What did he say about the problem of street children in South America?

9. What did he say were the main reasons?

10. What do people call these street children?

11. How does UNICEF help them? Give some examples.

II .Essay Writing

Write an essay by putting together the answers to the questions in Exercise I, using such joining words as because, and, but and so on.

III .Questions for Discussion

1. Why does the number of street children rise as a country becomes more urbanized? Is it also true in our country? Give facts.

2. What do you think we should do to help these children?

3. Have you noticed that the number of beggars in big cities is increasing in our country? Do you know why?

IV .Translation

Put the following Chinese into English, using as many as possible the phrases and expressions you have learned.

宋平是一位年輕的記者，他在重慶一家大報社工作。去年他花了近十個月的時間走了九個省，調查輟學兒童的狀況。調查結束後他寫了一篇報告，報告中說：這九個省的輟學兒童多達幾萬名，絕大部分的兒童都在8～16歲；女孩子比男孩子多，農村孩子比城市孩子多；在貧困地區這個問題更加嚴重。宋平說貧困是導致許多孩子退學的主要原因。在貴陽，他採訪了不少流浪街頭的兒童。他們大部分是中途退學的學生，他們當中的三分之二是來自貴州貧困山區的，剩下的是來自貴陽周邊城鎮的。他們來貴陽的目的是賺一點錢來補助家裡。在貴陽舉目無親，只能流浪街頭。有些孩子撿破爛，有些賣花賣報，有些擦皮鞋，其中有三男一女是從四川市永川區來的。他們的父母都是離婚後再婚的，由於在家裡常常挨打，他們就跑到貴陽，在那兒他們四人住在一幢爛尾樓裡，白天靠撿破爛賺錢，相依為命，互相保護。當問到今後的打算時，他們告訴宋平，他們還會繼續撿破爛，直到能賺很多錢，為那些街頭流浪兒辦一所學校。

Lesson 5   How New York Became America's Largest City

In the 18th century New York was smaller than Philadelphia and Boston. Today it is the largest city in America. How can the change in its size and importance be explained?

To answer this question we must consider certain facts about geography, history, and economics. Together these three will explain the huge growth of America's most famous city.

The map of the Northeast shows that four of the most heavily populated areas in this region are around seaports. At these points materials from across the sea enter the United States, and the products of the land are sent there for export across the sea. Economists know that places where transportation lines meet are good places for making raw materials into finished goods. That is why seaports often have cities nearby. But cities like New York needed more than their geographical location in order to become great industrial centers. Their development did not happen simply by chance.

About 1815, when many Americans from the east coast had already moved toward the west, trade routes from the ports to the central regions of the country began to be a serious problem. The slow wagons of that time, drawn by horses or oxen, were too expensive for moving heavy freight very far. Americans had long admired Europe's canals. In New York State a canal seemed the best solution to the transportation problem. From the eastern end of Lake Erie all the way across the state to the Hudson River there is a long strip of low land. Here the Erie Canal was constructed. After several years of work it was completed in 1825.

The canal produced an immediate effect. Freight costs were cut to about one-tenth of what they had been. New York City, which had been smaller than Philadelphia and Boston, quickly became the leading city of the coast. In the years that followed transportation routes on the Great Lakes were joined to routes on the Mississippi River. Then New York City became the end point of a great inland shipping system that extended from the Atlantic Ocean far up the western branches of the Mississippi.

The coming of the railroad made canal shipping less important, but it tied New York even more closely to the central regions of the country. It was easier for people in the central states to ship their goods to New York for export overseas.

Exports from New York were greater than imports. Consequently, shipping companies were eager to fill their ships with passengers on the return trip from Europe. Passengers could come from Europe very cheaply as a result.

Thus New York became the greatest port for receiving people from European countries. Many of these people remained in the city. Others stayed in New York for a few weeks, months, or years, and then moved to other parts of the United States. For these great numbers of new Americans New York had to provide homes, goods, and services. Their labor helped the city become great.

(499 words)

 Useful Phrases and Expressions

1. to answer this question we must consider certain facts about…

2. the huge growth of

3. the most heavily populated areas

4. transportation lines meet

5. make raw materials into finished goods

6. geographical location

7. The development did not happen simply by chance.

8. trade routes

9. central regions

10. Americans had long admired Europe's canals.

11. A canal seemed the best solution to...

12. After several years of work it was completed.

13. The canal produced an immediate effect.

14. Costs were cut to about one-tenth of what they had been.

15. the leading city of the coast

16. in the years that followed

17. The system extended from...to...

18. The coming of the railroads made canal shipping less important.

19. Exports from New York were greater than imports.

20. Their labor helped the city become great.

 Exercises

I .Comprehension Questions

1. Was New York City already the biggest city in the United States in the 18th century?

2. Is it the biggest city today?

3. How did the change happen?

4. Where is New York City?

5. What problem did people have in about 1815?

6. How did they solve this problem?

7. When was the canal completed?

8. What did the city benefit from the canal?

9. What happened in the years followed?

10. How did this help New York?

11. How did New York become the greatest port for receiving people from European countries?

12. Was this good for New York? Why?

II .Essay Writing

Write an essay by putting together the answers to the questions in Exercise I, using such joining words as because, and, but and so on.

III .Questions for Discussion

1. Do you like big cities? Why? What are the good things about them and what are the bad things about them?

2. How many cities are there in China now? Tell the history of one city's development.

IV .Translation

Put the following Chinese into English, using as many as possible the phrases and expressions you have learned.

1979 年之前，深圳還只是香港對岸的一個小漁村，然而今天它已成為一座人口超過千萬的現代化城市。深圳只用了 20 年多一點的時間就從一個窮村莊建設成為了一座現代化的大城市。當然這一切不是偶然的。它的地理位置、好的時機以及好的政府政策使得它能在 20 世紀末迅速發展成為一座最有名的城市。

　　深圳升格為城市是在 1979 年。它離香港很近，步行即可到香港。1978年後，香港商人到深圳投資辦公司變得十分容易。1992 年，鄧小平去深圳視察並對如何建設中國的市場經濟作了重要指示。此後中國政府給了深圳很多的自主權來發展城市經濟。市政府制定了很多優惠政策來吸引中國國內外的資金和人才。從此以後，深圳經濟迅猛發展。

　　為了加強和香港的聯繫，京九鐵路開工並於 1995 年全線通車。這樣深圳成為了鐵路、公路、海運和航空運輸的樞紐。依託於好的政策，去深圳工作的人有幾百萬，他們當中很多人就留在了深圳，為那裡的經濟建設做出了巨大的貢獻。

Lesson 6   Americans Rediscover Fitness in Their Feet

Put away the aerobic dance tights and the jogging suit. A less strenuous remedy for fat thighs and flabby bellies is becoming as chic as the high-fiber diet. It is called walking and it's the latest American fitness craze. Walking has been rediscovered as an activity that burns calories, trims the body and fortifies the heart. Last year, 30 million Americans pace through neighbourhoods, city streets and shopping malls regularly for exercise, according to a New York sports data firm.

And some 1.9 million Americans walk at least 48 kilometers a week. Already this breed of walkers, most of whom have never exercised before, outnumber the runners and tennis players, and nearly every other type of part-time athlete. A few are defectors from jogging and many are younger women who have shied away from rigorous exercise, or older folks whose doctors have told them to exercise to stay alive. They have transformed walking into a formal exercise by adding speed, time and a lot of sweat.

"The walking trend is at a stage now where running was in the early 1970s," said Harvey Lauer, of American Sports Data Inc., a Hartsdale, New York, firm that specializes in sports survey. "You can see joggers, but you can't see walkers," said Lauer.

In December, Urban Hiker—which bills itself "America's first walking store"—opened a shop in New York devoted exclusively to walking equipment. The owner, 27-year-old George Pakradoonia, told Reuters he came up with the idea while managing a more traditional shoes store for his father.

While walking has emerged as the latest fashion in fitness, exercise walking was first recommended years ago by cardiologists and other physicians to patients suffering from heart and lung disease, obesity and other health problems. Walking 1.6 kilometers at a pace of at least five kilometers an hour burns 100 calories. Exercise walking may also improve cardiovascular efficiency, lower blood pressure and reduce body fat, according to Dr. James Rippe, of the University of Massachusetts Medical Center.

Rippe, who does research for Rockport Co., found that walking at a brisk pace—fast enough to noticeably increase the heart rate—three times a week for 30 minutes can increase almost anyone's cardiovascular fitness by 15 percent.

Compared with running, exercise walking poses little risk of injury, according to several studies. In walking, the foot hits the pavement with a force 1.5 times the body weight.

With well-established health benefits and little risk, exercise walking appeals to a diverse group. In a recent survey by sports data, 40 to 50 percent of the 30 million Americans who called themselves exercise walkers were over 55 years old. In the same survey, 60 percent of the walkers were women. And 20 percent said they combined exercise walking with functional activities, such as going to work.

As the number of walkers has increased, activities to accommodate them have increased too. Walking clubs have sprouted up and walking marathons are held in Washington and San Francisco.

(497 words)

 Useful Phrases and Expressions

1. remedy for fat thighs and flabby bellies

2. high-fiber diet

3. fitness craze

4. burns calories, trims the body and fortifies the heart

5. outnumber

6. shy away from

7. rigorous exercise

8. They have transformed walking into a formal exercise by adding speed.

9. The walking trend is at a stage where...

10. devote exclusively to

11. come up with the idea

12. the latest fashion in fitness

13. health problems

14. improve cardiovascular efficiency, lower blood pressure, reduce body fat

15. increase heart rate

16. cardiovascular fitness

17. walk at a brisk pace

18. pose little risk of injury

19. well-established health benefits

20. appeal to a diverse group

21. combine exercise walking with functional activities

22. sprout up

 Exercises

I .Comprehension Questions

1. What has become the latest American fitness trend or craze?

2. How many people in the United States did exercise walking?

3. Who reported this number?

4. How many people are there, who walk at least 48 kilometers a week?

5. Who are these people? Why do they walk?

6. What have people rediscovered about walking?

7. Years ago who recommended walking?

8. Who did they recommend to?

9. Who is Dr. James Rippe?

10. What does he say about walking?

11. Why is exercise walking so popular with people?

12. What is the result of the increase of walkers?

II .Essay Writing

Write an essay by putting together the answers to the questions in Exercise I, using such joining words as because, and, but and so on.

III .Questions for Discussion

1. Do you believe what the text says about walking? Why?

2. What do you do to keep fit?

3. Do you think to keep fit is more important than to earn more money? Why?

IV .Translation

Put the following Chinese into English, using as many as possible the phrases and expressions you have learned.

古代醫書《黃帝內經》倡導人們走步健身治病。中國有兩句老話都是勸導人們走步的，一句是「人老先老腳」，另一句是「飯後百步走，能活九十九」。明清兩代的很多中醫積極主張用走步來治療很多慢性病。保健專家說，如果人們能做到每天走一萬步，那麼得心臟病、高血壓、糖尿病和肥胖病的人就會大大減少。現代醫學已證明走步能改善睡眠，因此醫生建議睡眠不好的病人在睡覺前步行半小時。

在歐洲，步行健身一直是十分流行的。很多歐洲國家在 60 年代就開始走步健身了。現在在法國有 3100 萬人參加走步健身，很多人喜歡徒步旅遊，所以很多旅行社推出徒步旅遊路線來滿足他們；在丹麥、德國，徒步旅遊變得很時尚；在英國、德國和法國，越來越多的人放棄了汽車而是步行上班，他們說步行上班不僅對他們的健康有益，而且也有利於保護環境。

Lesson 7   Family—For and Against

For...

There is a time when most young people in England feel they would like to leave home and live independently. Even though the break can be painful for both the parents being left and the young person who is leaving home, this attitude is respected.In some countries young people are not encouraged to leave home until they marry. In England we find this way of behaving rather suffocating. Many foreigners find our attitude to our families very cold. There should be a balance between these two attitudes. Certainly in England nowadays I don't think we realize the importance of the family and as a result there is a lot of unnecessary loneliness in every age group.

Some English children, especially boys, are sent to boarding school as young as seven. A lot of these people find they have problems in establishing close relationships when they get older as they never learned how to establish them with their families when they were young. A lot of old people feel they are a "nuisance" to their families and are very lonely because they are no longer needed. It's interesting to observe that in a society where families are not close there are a lot of organizations that cope with various social problems. In other countries it is the families who take care of each other, not organizations. I'm not saying that distant relationships with our families are the only reason for social problems but I feel close relationships would help.

Living independently is a good idea providing we are not too proud to go home when it's necessary. There are times when one cannot depend on one's friends and when one needs a place to go. We all need somewhere that we can be angry or upset and know that we'll still be loved. Family love should be unconditional. We should be accepted for what we are and forgiven for what we do. We should learn to use each other in times of stress and at the same time not expect each other to sacrifice our independence.

In these days of growing political and social insecurity the family should provide one of the few real stabilizing influences. It is a shelter that should be used positively and when it is necessary.

Against...

When we talk about the family we must make two important distinctions. Sociologists talk about the nuclear family, which means the small unit of parents and their children only and the extended family, which widens the distinction to include uncles, aunts, grandparents and all those other people that the British call distant relatives.

The extended family structure is more usual where people still live in villages or small towns and large family groups remain close to each other. Even when the members of the family have to go away to work, the family members are close to each other. In some industrialized societies people move away to other cities to study or work and they no longer keep close to their parents once they grow up.

But whether we are talking about the nuclear or the extended family, we can say that most people in families are tied together by obligation: what they must do for each other and how they should feel about each other.

When we are small we need the protection and care of our families and our parents do a lot for us. Parents usually decide to have children because they want them and so they have an obligation to look after that responsibility. But why must children be grateful for this? You should not have to be grateful for something which is your right.

People also say that parents and children must love each other. But when we grow up and can make our own choice we may find that we do not really like our families very much. There is a saying: "You can choose your friends but you cannot choose your family." And sometimes we like the friends we choose more than our relatives. This can hurt our families; they feel that their children are ungrateful and that they don't love them any more. The children feel angry because their parents disapprove of them or their friends, and want to tell them what to do with their lives. But both parents and children feel guilty when they hate those that they are supposed to love.

So families create cycles of duty, disappointment and guilt. And people must escape from that if they want to grow up fully.

(762 words)

 Useful Phrases and Expressions

1. There should be a balance between these two attitudes.

2. We find this way of behaving rather suffocating.

3. A lot of old people feel they are a nuisance to their families.

4. There are times when one cannot depend on one's friends...

5. Family love should be unconditional.

6. We should learn to use each other in times of stress.

7. distant relatives, close relatives

8. They have an obligation to look after that responsibility.

9. ...how they should feel about each other

10. The children feel angry that their parents disapprove of them or their friends.

11. So families create cycles of duty, disappointment and guilt.

12. People must escape from that if they want to grow up fully.

Exercises

I.Comprehension Questions

1. What do foreigners find people's relationship in England?

2. What causes this relationship? Can you explain?

3. What is the result of this kind of relationship?

4. Are there different attitudes towards the family?

5. What is the first one?

6. What are these people's arguments and their conclusion?

7. What is the other attitude towards the family?

8. What are these people's arguments and their conclusion?

II.Essay Writing

Write an essay by putting together the answers to the questions in Exercise I, using such joining words as because, and, but and so on.

III.Questions for Discussion

1. There are two attitudes towards the family in the text. Which one do you accept? What are your arguments?

2. Is the family very important to everyone? Why?

3. What role does the family play in our society?

4. Are there any changes in the attitude towards the family in China? What are they?

IV .Translation

Put the following Chinese into English, using as many as possible the phrases and expressions you have learned.

唐愛國在安徽省石台縣是位知名人士。他1996年畢業於北京農業大學。畢業後，北京一家大公司邀請他去公司工作，他沒有接受邀請，而是回到了家鄉石台。他的家鄉是安徽省最窮的村莊之一，他感到有義務和責任幫助家鄉脫貧致富。他的選擇得到了尊重，這樣他就被派回了家鄉工作。然而，頭幾個月日子十分艱難痛苦。大部分老鄉不理解他，他們認為唐愛國不是傻瓜就是在學校犯了錯。儘管他對村民講，他的指導和方法是沒有任何條件的，然而絕大部分村民還是不接受他的種田方法和指導。他感到十分失望，甚至有過要離開本村去江西省鳳陽的想法，那裡的農民相信他的方法，需要他的指導。他的幾個小學同學積極支持他留下。一年後情況發生了變化，幾家農戶使用了他的方法，接受了他的指導，賺的錢開始多起來了，生活也好多了。這下子剛開始時反對他的想法和方法的農民也都紛紛來求他幫忙。三年後，他們村和周圍幾個村都脫了貧，不少去城裡打工的年輕人也逐漸回來種地了。村民十分感激他的指導和奉獻，都選他當村長。他說在他困難的時候，他的朋友支持和鼓勵了他，不然他很可能已經離開了這裡去了鳳陽。

Lesson 8   The Language of Advertising

When we buy a product, we rarely think twice about its name. But a lot of time, money and effort go into choosing the right name for the right product. We visited Novamark International, a company that specializes in finding names for consumer products to see how complicated the process is.

John Murphy, Novamark's managing director, believes that a good brand name is crucial for a product's success. This is because it creates a personality that makes people regard a product in a particular way. For example, suppose the product in question is cheap family shampoo. If it is given an elegant, expensive sounding name, it would be inappropriate for the product and mislead the consumer. If it is given to feminine a name, some men may be reluctant to buy it. If it is given to "national" a name that makes us think of England, France or wherever, this could cause marketing problems in other countries.

Practical considerations have to be thought of as well. If the shampoo is to be sold in an upright plastic bottle, with the name on the front, then its name has to be short. It wouldn't make sense to have a long word that ran round the bottle, because it would be difficult to read. If a brand name is to be moulded onto a product, as with many soaps, the same sort of problem could arise.

The last 30 years has seen a massive growth in consumer products that all have to be checked when anything new comes onto the market. Novamark's approach to creating brand names is very sys tematic. The Novamark team includes trademark lawyers, psychologists, linguists, copywriters and marketing experts. These people, with the help of a word library and a computer, seek to create a brand name that is legible, memorable, pronounceable and with positive connotations in the countries where it is to be marketed.

Choosing a brand name in this scientific way shows us yet another important use of language. Some brand names, such as Biro, Hoover, have become so famous that they have been incorporated into the English language as nouns. Others, such as Coca Cola, are well known worldwide. Only one question remains to be asked and that is "Do we really need the consumer products the advertisers so skillfully persuade us to buy?"

What do you think?

(394 words)

 ## Useful Phrases and Expressions

1. think twice about

2. A lot of time, money and effort go into choosing the right name for the right product.

3. A good brand name is crucial for a product's success.

4. make people regard a product in a particular way

5. the product in question

6. be reluctant to do sth.

7. It would (wouldn't) make sense to do something.

8. The last 30 years has seen a massive growth in...

9. The approach is very systematic.

10. positive connotations

11. The same sort of problem could arise.

12. Only one question remains to be asked and that is...

 Exercises

I .Comprehension Questions

1. What place did the writer and his friends visit?

2. What did they find? Why?

3. Why is that a good brand name is crucial for a product's success?

4. What is the another thing, which is also important to a brand name?

5. What has happened in the last 30 years?

6. What does the writer and his friends think of Novamark's approach to creating brand names?

7. What name is considered a good brand name?

8. How famous are brand names like Biro and Hoover?

9. What is one question that remains to be asked?

II .Essay Writing

Write an essay by putting together the answers to the questions in Exercise I, using such joining words as because, and, but and so on.

III .Questions for Discussion

1. Do you think the language of advertisement is crucial?

2. Find some advertisements in which you think the language is not good. As a result, the advertisement may mislead the customers or make them reluctant to buy them.

IV .Translation

Put the following Chinese into English, using as many as possible the phrases and expressions you have learned.

中國沒有航空母艦。20多年來，人們一直在討論中國是否應該有自己的航空母艦，有兩種意見：一種認為，中國當然應該有自己的航母；另一種認為，沒有必要擁有航母。贊同的人認為，中國是世界上最大的國家之一，理應有自己的航母。在過去25年中，世界各國的軍事裝備都有了巨大的發展，一些以前沒有航母的國家現在已經有了。他們擁有航母的目的是防衛，保衛自己的領海和海岸。中國的海岸線長達18400公里，需要保衛自己的領海和海岸。

但不同意的人認為，沒有必要有自己的航母。他們的主要理由是：中國還沒有富到可以造多艘航母。因為建造這艘巨船需要投入大量的時間、財力和人力，而中國還有很多問題急需解決。要解決這些問題同樣需要時間、財力和人力。要造一艘航母要花上幾十個億，由於材料費在不斷的上漲，建造船的費用同步也要上漲。還有一個很實際的問題必須考慮，那就是：使用航母的費用要遠遠超出建造它的費用。一艘航母的壽命為30年，這30年中的費用需要400～500億。因此必須先問一個問題：「為了保衛領海和海岸，我們真的必須花那麼多錢來造航母嗎？」

Lesson 9 The Motor Car—a Boom or a Menace

The use of the motor car is becoming more and more widespread in the twentieth century. As an increasing number of countries develop both technically and economically, a larger proportion of the world's population is able to buy and use a car. Possessing a car gives a much greater degree of mobility, enabling the driver to move around freely. The owner of a car is no longer forced to work locally. He can choose from a greater variety of jobs and probably changes his work more frequently as he is not restricted to a choice within a small radius. Traveling to work by car is also more comfortable than having to use public transport; the driver can adjust the heating in winter and the air-conditioning in the summer to suit his own needs and preference. There is no irritation caused by waiting for trains, buses or underground trains, standing in long patient queues, or sitting on draughty platforms, for as long as half an hour sometimes. With the building of good fast motorways long distances can be covered rapidly and pleasantly. For the first time in this century also, many people are now able to enjoy their leisure time to the full by making trips to the country or seaside at the weekends, instead of being confined to their immediate neighbourhood. This feeling of independence, and the freedom to go where you please, is perhaps the greatest advantage of the car.

When considering the drawbacks, perhaps pollution is of prime importance. As more and more cars are produced and used, the emissions from their exhaust pipes contains ever larger volume of poison ous gas. Some of the contents of this gas, such as lead, not only pollute the atmosphere but cause actual harm to the health of people. Many of the minor illnesses of modern industrial society, headaches, tiredness, and stomach upsets are thought to arise from breathing polluted air. Doctors' surgeries are full of people suffering from illnesses caused by pollution. It is also becoming increasingly difficult to deal with the problem of traffic in towns. Most of the important cities of the world suffer from traffic congestion. In fact, any advantage gained in comfort is often cancelled out in cities by the frustration caused by traffic jams, endless queues of cars crawling bumper to bumper through all the main streets. As an increasing number of traffic regulation schemes are devised, the poor bewildered driver finds himself diverted and forced into one-way systems which cause even greater delays than the traffic jams they are supposed to prevent. The soaring cost of petrol and the increased license fees and road tax all add to the driver's worries. In fact, he must sometimes wonder if the motorcar is such a boom, or just a menace.

(463 words)

 Useful Phrases and Expressions

1. The use of the motor car is becoming more and more widespread.

2. an increasing number of

3. Possessing a car gives a much greater degree of mobility.

4. rely on public transport

5. work locally

6. He can choose from a greater variety of jobs.

7. changes one's job/work frequently

8. adjust the heating in winter and the air-conditioning in the summer

9. suit one's own needs and preference

10. There is no irritation caused by...

11. Long distances can be covered rapidly and pleasantly.

12. be confined to

13. this feeling of independence and the freedom to go where you please

14. the drawbacks

15. Pollution is of prime importance.

16. the minor illness of modern industrial society

17. It is also becoming increasingly difficult to deal with the problem of...

18. The advantage is often cancelled out by...

19. Cars are crawling bumper to bumper through all the main streets.

20. the soaring cost of petrol

21. All add to the driver's worries.

 Exercises

I .Comprehension Questions

1. What does possessing a car give?

2. Why do we say that the driver has a lot of freedom when having a car?

3. Why do we say that the driver has a lot of comfort when having a car?

4. How have good fast motorways helped?

5. What else can people do with their cars?

6. Are there any drawbacks of having cars?

7. What is the biggest problem of cars?

8. How do cars cause harm to the health of people?

9. What is another big problem of cars?

10. Is this problem very serious?

11. Is it difficult to deal with this problem?

12. What is the trouble with one-way systems?

13. What do people sometimes think of cars?

II .Essay Writing

Write an essay by putting together the answers to the questions in Exercise I, using such joining words as because, and, but and so on.

III .Questions for Discussion

1. Are you for the writer's analysis of having cars? Can you give your own facts about the advantages and disadvantages of cars?

2. Should our government encourage people to buy cars? Why?

3. Should our country develop automobile industry? Why?

IV .Translation

Put the following Chinese into English, using as many as possible the phrases and expressions you have learned.

從 1990 年起，到蘇州開公司、開工廠的外商越來越多。他們感到蘇州是個投資的好地方，因為投資所受限制少，地方政府辦事效率高，並能幫助他們解決問題。蘇州的地理位置也很好：蘇州到上海這段距離，開車走高速公路只需一個小時，從市中心到南京走高速公路乘小型車或巴士只需兩個半小時，乘火車只需用三個小時；蘇州到上海虹橋國際機場開車不到一個小時。

蘇州的物價要比上海、北京便宜。蘇州菜很好吃而且品種多。出外很方便，可乘公共汽車，也可以騎自行車。儘管蘇州城不大，但你也不會感到沒有地方去。週末和節日能去的地方很多。中國最大的湖──太湖，離蘇州開車只有 45 分鐘車程。湖內有很多島嶼，你和朋友或家人可以去那裡，一定會玩得很痛快。

蘇州唯一的不足之處是夏天熱，冬天冷，冬天屋裡沒有暖氣。不過這不會使很多外商感到煩惱，因為現在蘇州使用空調越來越普遍了。很多當地居民家裡都有空調，冬天開暖氣，夏天開冷氣。然而，最近幾年汽車數量大增，交通擁擠，使出外交通越來越困難。上下班到處堵車，很使人惱火。如果不馬上解決這個問題，一些優勢條件會讓交通擁擠給抵消了。

Lesson 10   Does Tobacco Make Economic Sense?

Smoking kills millions of people each year, says the World Health Organization, but for the hundred or so developing countries that grow the crop, tobacco has been considered a paying proposition. Recent evidence suggests, however, that tobacco makes poor economic sense for both producing countries and its growers.

In 1998, the worldwide production of tobacco leaf was 6.27 million tons, and there are now stocks of 7.19 million tons in hand—in other words, more than a year's output. This massive quantity is far larger than the equivalent stocks of any other agricultural commodity, which is an indication that tobacco prices are likely to stay low.

The world tobacco price today is around 20 percent less in real terms than it was in 1995. Earnings by the exporting countries will continue to be under pressure. Moreover, smoking related disease is growing in many countries and the cost of disease has to be offset against tobacco's returns. Studies for African countries have yet to be done, but work in Canada by W.E. Forbes and M.E. Thompson at University Waterloo refutes the idea that tobacco is beneficial to economies of producing countries.

Their study found that Canadians spent $4.4 billion in 1998 on tobacco products. But the costs of smoking, such as physicians' fee, hospital bills, drugs and administrative services, came to $7.1 billion. Canada therefore loses $2.7 billion a year on its tobacco industry, they concluded.

The Economist Intelligence Unit in London points out that tobacco productivity in the developing countries is generally low—averaging around 1,000 kilograms per hectare. One investigation in Kenya found that tobacco farmers earned less than 150 pounds sterling a year from their plots, which was only about two-thirds of what coffee farmers were earning from similar sized plots.

The environmental cost of growing tobacco is heavy, too, the researchers found. Over half the world's tobacco leaf is cured in wood barns and an enormous volume of wood is needed for this process. According to a study of peasant tobacco farming in Tanzania, on average the wood from between two and three hectares of land is needed to cure one ton of tobacco. Thus, many thousands of hectares of scarce African forest are going up in smoke to make cigarettes.

Moreover, food output is threatened by tobacco growing. In the Meru district of Kenya, for example, people say that rainfall has declined since tobacco was introduced 25 years ago. Trees that once protected good food-growing land have now gone, thus putting in jeopardy that land's ability to produce food.

 Useful Phrases and Expressions

1. Tobacco has been considered a paying proposition.

2. Recent evidence suggests that...

3. Tobacco makes poor economic sense.

4. producing countries and the growers

5. There are now stocks of...tons in hand.

6. agricultural commodity

7. It is an indication that...

8. Prices are likely to stay low.

9. Earnings by the exporting countries will continue to be under pressure.

10. Smoking related disease is growing.

11. The cost of disease has to be offset against tobacco's returns.

12. Their study found that...

13. The environmental cost of growing tobacco is heavy.

14. An enormous volume of wood is needed for...

15. Food output is threatened by...

16. Rainfall has declined.

17. good food-growing land

18. in jeopardy

 Exercises

I .Comprehension Questions

1. What does the World Health Organization say about smoking?

2. What do a lot of developing countries think of growing tobacco?

3. What does recent evidence show?

4. What was the worldwide production of tobacco leaf in 1998?

5. How big are the stocks now?

6. What does this indicate?

7. What is the world tobacco price?

8. What is growing in many countries?

9. Why is tobacco not beneficial to the economies of producing countries?

10. What does a study say about tobacco productivity in developing countries?

11. Why is it that growing tobacco is bad for the environment?

12. What is the more serious thing?

II .Essay Writing

Write an essay by putting together the answers to the questions in Exercise I, using such joining words as because, and, but and so on.

III .Questions for Discussion

1. Who smokes in China? Why do they smoke? Do you smoke?Why?

2. Do you think our country should cut down tobacco production? What are your reasons?

IV .Translation

Put the following Chinese into English, using as many as possible the phrases and expressions you have learned.

禽流感在中國已經過去了。在過去六個月裡中國宰殺了近九百萬隻雞鴨，亞洲其他國家共宰殺了約三千萬隻，因此在亞洲對雞鴨的需求很快就會增加。這就意味著雞鴨的價格會很快上漲。最近的跡象已表明現在多養雞鴨是個賺錢的買賣。

在禽流感期間，我的壓力很大，怕禽流感會傳染到我養的雞鴨。幸運的是，牠們都安然無恙。可有幾次我真想把農場賣了，因為成本太高，難以把本錢賺回來，飼養的成本遠遠高出賣出的錢。此外，我還有一家雞鴨飼料場，生意不好，在禽流感之前產品可出口到很多國家，賺了不少錢。但禽流感期間，飼料價格和以前相比跌了 30%，我向銀行借的錢也沒還。我的生意受到了很大的威脅。我也不知道禽流感什麼時候才能過去，我的生意已被它逼到做不下去的地步了。現在一切都過去了，生意好起來了，再過三個月，我欠的錢差不多就可以全部還清了。

Lesson 11   The Sale of Council Houses

Nearly one third of all the houses in Britain are rented from local authorities. This proportion is higher than in any other western European countries. Altogether about seven million houses and flats throughout the country are owned in this way. The local authorities rent the houses and flats to people who cannot afford to buy their own homes. Recently the Conservative government has decided to encourage the sale of these houses (council houses as they are known) to tenants who want to buy them and can afford to pay. But this idea has caused a lot of debate in Britain. Here we look at some of the arguments for and against the sale of council houses.

The Conservative Party

The Conservative government does not want to sell all council houses. It sees that in some areas and for some people this kind of housing is the best answer. But the Conservative government believes that too many houses in Britain are owned by local authorities and that this is bad for the country, especially the economy. Their argument is that an essential part of a healthy economy is a workforce which is mobile, which is able to move to wherever it is needed. But the worker who lives in a council house finds it difficult to move because there may be no council houses vacant in the area he wants to move to. According to some economists this has been one reason why in some areas there are job vacancies but no one has moved to these areas to take up the jobs.

A second Conservative criticism of council housing is that this kind of housing receives a large subsidy from the government's funds. As we are now going through a period of economic need, the government sees the sale of council houses as one way of saving money by doing away with the subsidy.

The third Conservative argument is more political. By encouraging people to own their homes the Conservative government aims to create a country in which the vast majority of people will own their own homes. Selling council houses to tenants is seen as one way to achieve this aim.

For these reasons the Conservative government has decided that anyone who has been a council house tenant for three years or more has the right to buy his home from the local authority. Also those people who have been tenants for many years and who now decide to buy their houses will be able to buy them for less than the market value.

This scheme has already been introduced in some areas and over 42,000 houses have been sold to tenants.

The Labour Party

The main opposition party in Britain, the Labour Party, is very much against the sale of council houses.

The Labour Party argues that the sale of council houses will make it more difficult for poor families to get a home of their own in any area where there is already a shortage of houses. They say that poor people will not be able to rent council houses because these council houses will have already been sold.

A second Labour argument is that only the best council houses will be sold. This will mean that the local authority will have only the worst houses left for rent. So poor people will have to live in the worst houses, and will have little chance of moving to a nicer council house.

Another Labour argument is that the sale of council houses amounts to selling community assets at low prices. They feel that council houses should not be sold while there are people without houses, because the cost to the community of building new council houses now is much greater than when the existing houses were built.

What do you think? Should people be able to own their own houses or is it better to have a large number of houses available to be let at low rents? Do people in your country buy their houses or do they rent them? Do you have "council houses" in your country?

(681 words)

 ## Useful Phrases and Expressions

1. local authorities

2. This proportion is high.

3. This idea has caused a lot of debate in…

4. It needs that…

5. This kind of housing is the best answer.

6. This is bad for the country, especially the economy.

7. A healthy economy is a workforce which is mobile.

8. job vacancies

9. This kind of housing receives a large subsidy from…

10. the government funds

11. aim to create a country in which the vast majority of people

12. Selling council houses to tenants is seen as one way to achieve this aim.

13. the market value

14. do away with subsidy

15. This scheme has already been introduced in some areas.

16. The Labor Party is very much against the sale of council houses.

17. There is already a shortage of...

18. have little chance of

19. The sale of council house amounts to selling community assets at low prices.

20. existing houses

 Exercises

I .Comprehension Questions

1. In Britain how many houses are rented from local authorities?

2. Is this proportion low or high in Europe?

3. What has the Conservative government decided to do?

4. How many reasons do they have?

5. What is their first reason?

6. What is their second reason?

7. What is their last reason?

8. Are the houses the tenants can buy very expensive?

9. What is the attitude of the Labor Party to this idea?

10. Do they have reasons? How many?

11. What is their first reason?

12. What is their second reason?

13. What is their third reason?

II .Essay Writing

Write an essay by putting together the answers to the questions in Exercise I, using such joining words as because, and, but and so on.

III .Questions for Discussion

1. Do you know the housing system in our country? Is it good? Why?

2. Is it possible that every family in our country can own their own house? Why? What should the government do?

3. Do you want to own your own house when you have a family? How are you going to do that?

IV .Translation

Put the following Chinese into English, using as many as possible the phrases and expressions you have learned.

中國農業的形勢很嚴峻，這使大家感到很焦急。我們就拿糧食生產為例，過去的幾年裡糧食生產每年都在減產。中國每年需消耗 5 億噸糧食，然而每年的糧食產量都在 4.2 億～ 4.5 億之間，每年缺口達 5000 萬～ 8000 萬噸，政府只能動用儲備糧來拉平缺口，這不是良策。有人說，我們可以從其他產糧國家多進口些糧食，這也不是個好辦法。如果中國多進口糧食，那麼世界糧價就會上漲。唯一的辦法就是鼓勵農民多種糧。

那麼是什麼原因使糧食產量下降呢？原因主要有兩個：第一個原因是，很多好的耕地被地方官員賣了，不少是低價賣掉的。中國正處在城市化的進程中，很多農田被用來建設城鎮，這也無可非議。但有不少好耕地沒有得到合理的使用，每年用於種糧的農田都在減少。第二個原因是農民都認為種糧不賺錢，結果越來越多的農民放棄了種糧。

溫家寶總理說，中國政府決心要解決農業問題，已頒布了鼓勵農民種糧的措施。在今後 5 年內要取消農業稅；為了增加種糧農民的收入，政府要提

高了糧價,加大農業補助;同時,大量的好農田要歸還給農民。越來越多的
農民看到了種糧有利,因此今年的糧食生產一定會增加的。

Lesson 12   Self-Medication

Occasional self-medication has always been part of normal living. The making and selling of drugs has a long history and is closely linked, like medical practice itself, with belief in magic. Only during the last hundred years or so has the development of scientific techniques made it possible for some of the causes of symptoms to be understood, so that more accurate diagnosis of many illnesses can be made with specific treatment of their causes. In many other illnesses, of which the causes remain unknown, it is still limited, like the unqualified prescriber, to the treatment of symptoms. The doctor is trained to decide when to treat symptoms only and when to attack the cause: this is an essential difference between medical prescribing and self-medication.

The advance of technology has brought about great progress in some fields of medicine, including the development of scientific drug therapy. In many countries public health organization is improving, and people's nutrition standards have risen. Paralleled with such beneficial trends are two which have an adverse effect. One is the use of high pressure advertising by the pharmaceutical industry, which has tended to influence both patients and doctors. This has led to the overuse of drugs generally. The other is the emergence of the sedentary society with its faulty ways of life: lack of exercise, over-eating, unsuitable eating, insufficient sleep, excessive smoking and drinking. People with disorders arising from faulty habits such as these, as well as from unhappy human relationships, often resort to selfmedication and so add the taking of pharmaceuticals to the list. Ad vertisers go to great lengths to catch this market.

Clever advertising aims at chronic sufferers who will try anything because doctors have not been able to cure them. It can induce such faith in a preparation, particularly if steeply priced. That will produce—by suggestion—a very real effect in some people. Advertisements are also aimed at people suffering from mild complaints such as simple colds and coughs, which clear up by themselves within a short time.

These are the main reasons why indigestion remedies, painkillers, cough mixtures, tonics, vitamins and iron tablets, nosedrops, ointments and many other preparations are found in quantity in many households. It is doubtful whether taking these things ever improves a person's health; it may even make it worse. Worse because the preparation may contain unsuitable ingredients; worse because the taker may become dependent on them; worse because they might be taken in excess; worse because they may cause poisoning, and worst of all because symptoms of some serious underlying cause may be masked and therefore medical help may not be sought. Selfdiagnosis is a greater danger than self-medication.

(443 words)

 ## Useful Phrases and Expressions

1. Self-medication has always been part of normal living.

2. be closely linked with

3. sth.has made it possible for sth./sb.to do...

4. He is limited to...

5. treat symptoms; attack the cause

6. The advance of technology has brought about much progress.

7. drug therapy

8. public health

9. People's nutrition standards have risen.

10. adverse effect

11. sedentary society

12. faulty ways of life

13. people with disorders

14. lack of exercise, over-eating, unsuitable eating, insufficient sleep, excessive smoking and drinking

15. to go to great lengths to do sth.

16. to catch the market

17. aim at

18. chronic sufferers

19. if steeply priced

20. produce a very real effect in

21. It is doubtful whether...

22. become dependent on

23. take sth.in excess

24. Underlying causes may be masked.

25. medical help

26. self-diagnosis

 Exercises

I .Comprehension Questions

1. What has always been part of normal living?

2. What has made it possible for people to understand some of the causes of illnesses?

3. What has the advance of technology made available?

4. But at the same time what has the advance of technology also created?

5. What is the first problem?

6. What is the second problem?

7. What is the dangerous thing about self-medication?

II .Essay Writing

Write an essay by putting together the answers to the questions in Exercise I, using such joining words as because, and, but and so on.

III .Questions for Discussion

1. Do you do self-medication sometimes?

2. Do you think it necessary for people to know something about medication? Why?

3. Do you think in the future more and more people will do selfmedication? Why?

IV .Translation

Put the following Chinese into English, using as many as possible the phrases and expressions you have learned.

前幾年，洪昭光醫生做過多次有關如何保持健康的報告，每次都十分成功。去聽他報告的有各種年齡段的人。他說現在醫學很發達，公共衛生水準在不斷地提高，人們的營養也比以前好了，現在人的壽命要比四五十年前長得多。因此人們可以輕鬆活到 100 歲，這已不是夢想。然而，與此同時，現在有另一種趨勢使健康專家們感到擔憂。根據一項調查，一半以上的城市居

民，特別是大城市的居民都患有慢性疾病，如高血壓、心臟病、肥胖症、糖
尿病等。讓人更擔憂的是，越來越多的年輕人得這些病。一旦患上了這些病，
他們就永遠斷不了根。洪醫生說引起這些疾病的主要原因是久坐不動，加上
不良的生活方式，如缺乏運動、飲食過量、飲食不當、缺乏睡眠、煙酒過量等。
過去人們騎自行車上班，現在越來越多的人開車上班，去辦公室也不是走著
去而是乘電梯。他們常常在電腦前一坐就是一天，晚餐大吃一頓，吃的食物
都是高蛋白、高脂肪、高鹽、高糖的東西。飯後馬上坐著看電視直到半夜。
有些人睡前還吃宵夜。這就是為什麼那麼多的城裡人身體都有毛病的原因。
洪醫生說，要健康一定要改變現在不良的生活方式，多運動並要改變飲食習
慣，少吃肉多吃蔬菜水果，喝綠茶遠比喝可口可樂之類的飲料要好得多。

Lesson 13   What do Parents Owe Their Children?

If I had to select a word that best describes the majority of American parents, that word would be guilt-ridden. Every day I receive an unending stream of mail and each family has a different story to tell. But the message is almost always the same: "We blew it."

Beleaguered Mom and Dad tell me they did their best but "something went wrong." How sad it is to see parents become the willing victims of the "give-me game," only to discover that no matter what they do, it isn't enough. Love's magic spell may be everywhere, but when you try to buy it, the price goes up, as it does with any other commodity. In the end, parents are despised for their lack of firmness and blamed when their spoiled children get into trouble. With this in mind, I shall first answer the question: "what do parents owe their children?" and I shall start with what they don't owe them.

Parents don't owe their children every minute of their day and every ounce of their energy. They don't owe them round-the-clock car service, singing lessons, tennis lessons, summer camp, ski outfits and ten-speed bicycles, a Honda or a car when they turn sixteen, or a trip to Europe when they graduate from high school.

I take the firm position that parents do not owe their children a college education.If their children are serious students and have well-defined goals, fine, send them to college if they can afford it. But parents must not feel guilty if they can't. If the children really want to go, they'll find a way. There are plenty of loans and scholarships for the bright and eager who can't afford to pay.

After children marry, their parents do not owe them a down payment on a house or money for the furniture. Parents do not have an obligation to baby-sit their kids or take over when they are on vacation. If the parents want to do any of these things, it should be considered an act of generosity, not an obligation.

In my opinion, parents do not owe their children an inheritance, no matter how much money they have. One of the surest ways to produce loafers is to let children know that their future is assured. At this point, you're probably wondering whether parents owe their children anything. My answer is, yes, they owe them a great deal.

One of their chief obligations is to give their children a sense of personal worth, for self-esteem is the basis of good mental health. A youngster who is continually criticized and "put down", made to feel stupid and unworthy, constantly compared with brighter brothers, sisters or cousins will not try to improve. On the contrary, he/she will become so unsure, so terrified of failing that he won't try at all. The child who is repeatedly called "bad" or "naughty" or "no good" will have such a low opinion of himself—of herself that he/she will behave in a way that justifies the parents' description.

Of course they should be corrected when they do wrong— this is the way children learn. But the criticisms should be heavily outweighed by praise. To a child, parents are the most important people in the world. Pleasing them and looking good in their eyes is the greatest satisfaction. To fail them is the worst punishment of all. Some parents find it difficult to verbalize approval of their children, even though they do think well of them. Parents who cannot praise with words should show their approval in other ways—with a smile or a hug. No child is ever too old to be hugged.

Parents owe their children consistency in discipline and firm guidelines. It is frightening for a youngster to feel that he is in charge of himself; it's like being in a car with no brakes. Even a very young child is aware that discipline is a special kind of love. When you say, "No, you can't go," he may put on a long face, but deep down he will be greatly relieved. The parent who says "No" when the other parent says "Yes" sends a double message. He is also saying: "I love you, and I am ready to risk your anger, because I don't want you to get into trouble."

Parents owe their children privacy and respect for their personal belongings. This means not borrowing things without permission, not reading diaries and mail, not looking through purses, pockets, and drawers. If a mother feels that she must read her daughter's diary to know what is going on, the communication between them must be pretty bad.

Parents owe their children a set of decent standards and solid values around which to build their lives. This means teaching them to respect the rights and opinions of others; it means being respectful to elders, to teachers, and to the law. The best way to teach such values is by example. When parents keep their promises, no matter what the cost, they teach their children the importance of honoring a commitment. A child who is lied to will lie. A child who sees his parents steal tools from the factory or towels from a hotel will think that it is all right to steal. A child who is slapped and punched will slap and punch others. A youngster who hears no laughter and sees no love in the home will have a difficult time laughing and loving.

No child asks to be born. If you bring a life into the world, you owe the child something. And if you give him his due, he'll have something of value to pass along to your grandchildren.

(957 words)

Useful Phrases and Expressions

1. have a different story to tell

2. willing victims of

3. only to discover (find) that

4. No matter what they do, it isn't enough.

5. lack of firmness

6. I shall start with... (n.) / (a clause)

7. I take the firm position that...

8. a serious student

9. well-defined goals

10. There are plenty of loans and scholarship for the bright and eager.

11. a down payment on

12. have an obligation to do sth.

13. one of the surest ways to

14. The future is assured.

15. at this point

16. give their children a sense of personal worth

17. Self-esteem is the basis of good mental health.

18. have a low/high/good/bad opinion of oneself

19. in one's eyes

20. think well of sb.

21. put on a long face

22. deep down

23. a double message

24. a set of decent standards and solid values around which to build their lives

25. be respectful to elders, to teachers, and to the law

26. to teach by example

27. give sb. his due

 Exercises

I .Comprehension Question

1. What dose the writer receive every day?

2. What do the majority of the parents say?

3. What is the beleaguered parents' problem?

4. What does the writer think is the cause? Why?

5. What is the writer's strong opinion about what the parents owe their children? Why?

6. But should they owe their children anything?

7. What is one of their chief obligations?

8. What should they do when their children do wrong?

9. How should they deal with criticism and praise?

10. Why should parents constantly discipline their children and give them firm guidelines?

11. Should parents respect their children's privacy?

12. What is another important obligation for parents to do? Why?

13. What is the best way to teach children?

14. If parents give their children their due, what will happen?

II .Essay Writing

Write an essay by putting together the answers to the questions in Exercise I, using such joining words as because, and, but and so on.

III .Questions for Discussion

1. Do you share the same views with the writer about family education?

2. Do you want to have a child in the future? How would you educate your child?

3. Why is it that nowadays many parents spoil their children? Is it necessary to help these parents? How?

IV .Translation

Put the following Chinese into English, using as many as possible the phrases and expressions you have learned.

　　有一件事十分有意思，聚會時大部分人都會談論孩子。他們常會訴苦，不管為孩子做多少事，孩子總不領情。每個家庭都有一本難念的經。孩子在學校常出事，倒霉的是家長，有些孩子花錢像百萬富翁。有一次，一位中學教師告訴我說，一些孩子花錢的派頭很嚇人。他有一個學生才 13 歲，過生日花了 2600 元，可是他還生他父母的氣，原因是他覺著生日派對不夠氣派。這個孩子的家長告訴這位老師說，他盡力要把孩子的生日辦得體面一些，但到頭來還是落了埋怨。中國的孩子給慣壞了。這僅僅是一個例子。

　　我堅信中國的家庭教育出了問題。現在孩子的問題各種各樣的都有。大部分的問題都是由於家庭教育不好而造成的。很多家長對孩子管教不嚴，不對孩子進行價值觀和自尊方面的教育。我發現有些孩子不尊老、尊師和尊重朋友，原因是他們的父母也不尊老和尊重他人。有這樣一個人，他常常因為一些小事和鄰居打架，他的兩個兒子也常和其他孩子打架。每次兩個兒子做了壞事他非但不教育他們，反而總是設法幫助他們隱瞞或逃避。這位父親是在毀他兩個兒子的前途。中國優秀文化中有極好的教誨，現在該是我們的學校和家長用這些教誨來教育孩子的時候了。

Lesson 14   Japan's Education System

As usual at this time of year, with school summer holidays over, the weather bureau, national science museum and many other Japanese institutions were crowded with researchers seeking answers to vacation assignments. But for disillusion officials it was a most depressing sight. The usual questions were being asked, of course— but the bright young faces of students eager for knowledge have been replaced by the earnest ones of their mothers.

"Before, the children always came to research for their homework. But now it's almost invariably the mothers, or even the fathers who come, while the kids stay home and take it easy," lamented a weather bureau official. This phenomenon reveals two things about contemporary Japan:

1. The over protectiveness of Japanese mothers is reaching ridiculous proportions.

2. Children have lost the interest in an education system that turns them into mere passive vessels for the intake of necessary information to pass examinations.

The image that has been built up of post-war Japan's education is of a treadmill in which there are very clear distinctions between winners and losers. The winners go onwards, passing the extremely stiff, highly competitive entrance examination at every stage of school life in order to get into the right university, which will ensure employment by the right (i.e.big) company—even if it is merely a job as an office clerk.

The losers in this juvenile rat race bear the scars and stigma of failure for life.

Hence, there have been tremendous pressures on youngsters here to succeed at any cost. Those who do fail tend to overreact, providing vital raw material for the frightening rises in juvenile delinquency and suicide.

The government has tried to introduce reforms to lessen the damaging effects of the heated-up competition—the so-called examination hell—without actually tampering with the core of the sterile system. There was nationwide astonishment recently when the Osakas prefectural board of education revealed the results of survey showing students were more interested in sex, music, clothes and sports than in studying.

The survey found seven of ten students unhappy with their studies. One third said they could do better but didn't feel like making the efforts. Six of ten did no homework, and one of three said he or she had considered dropping out of high school altogether.

The most significant finding of all was that 80% of students interviewed were not unduly concerned about the future of seeking fame or fortune.

A depressing picture emerged from the survey of a stereotyped education system unable to respond to students'needs. The report insisted that the youngsters were not lacking in ambition or desire to learn, but showed little interest in independent effort (having been spoonfed at home and school for so long) and were ready to blame their poor results on others.

A Japan Youth Research Institute study shows that high school students who either are lethargic or overly studious, do not enjoy their school life and have few friends of the opposite sex.

The Education Ministry, in its report for fiscal 1995 said Japanese schoolchildren today, under the heavy regime of all work and no play, are thin, shortsighted, in poor health generally and prone to tooth decay. And then there is the report of the national police agency showing that juvenile delinquency last year reached a postwar high with a statistical 13.6 out of every 1000 minors involved in an indictable crime.

A confusion in sense of values and the crumbling of social and family values is making children lose their sense of right and wrong in Japan's most affluent era ever. That is the official explanation, which comes back ultimately to an education problem. The biggest single factor in the mostly mindless crimes of theft and violence was reaction to failure at school. Most worrying is the increasing involvement of girls. The number of them taken into protective custody is 2.7 times the 1990 figure including a 74.7 percent increase in drug abuse.

Finally, there is the figure of suicides for the first half of this year: 521, an increase of 68 over the same period last year. This is the ultimate dropout that no system can tolerate.

(695 words)

 Useful Phrases and Expressions

1. at this time of year

2. It was a most depressing sight.

3. be replaced by

4. The kids stay home and take it easy.

5. The over protectiveness of Japanese mothers is reaching ridiculous proportions.

6. lose interest in

7. There are very clear distinctions between winners and losers.

8. at every stage of school life

9. rat race

10. at any cost

11. lessen the damaging effects of...

12. heated-up competition

13. seven of ten students

14. They didn't feel like making the efforts.

15. The most significant finding of... is (was) that

16. seek fame and fortune

17. respond to students' needs

18. independent effort

19. blame their poor results on others

20. to be prone to

21. mindless crimes of

22. most worrying is

 Exercises

I .Comprehension Questions

1. How can you describe Japan's education systems in one sentence?

2. What happens to the winners?

3. What about the losers?

4. What does a study by Japan Youth Research Institute show?

5. What picture does another survey show?

6. Is the education system able to respond to the students' needs?

7. Why do one third of students want to drop out of school?

8. What is their attitude towards homework?

9. How many of the students want to drop out of school?

10. What did Education Ministry say in its 1995 report about the school children today?

11. What is the most worrying thing?

12. What is the suicide figure in the first half of the year?

13. Has the government done anything to solve the problems?

14. What are the results? Why?

II .Essay Writing

Write an essay by putting together the answers to the questions in Exercise I, using such joining words as because, and, but and so on.

III .Question for Discussion

1. Based on your personal experience make some comments on the education system. Give examples.

2. To your mind what is a good education system? Why do you think so?

3. Can you make some good suggestions about how to improve the teaching quality?

IV .Translation

Put the following Chinese into English, using as many as possible the phrases and expressions you have learned.

中國的中小學教育怎麼了？一些教育家對 20 個省的中小學做了一項調查，看到了那裡的教育情況，從調查中發現了一個很讓人傷心的現象。他們發現，學生的書包越來越沉，在學校的時間越來越長，假期越來越短。很多學生在星期六、星期天還要上學。學生作業負擔太重，根本沒有時間玩耍。高中學生壓力更大，因為要參加大學入學考，這種考試難而死板，競爭很激烈。80% 的高三學生說他們每天只睡五六個小時，沒有假日。這種競爭越來越厲害，造成很多不良影響。這種影響產生了三大問題：

一、很多學生對學習失去了興趣，他們感到自己成為老師灌輸知識的容器，而這些知識僅僅是為了考試。結果造成大量的學生輟學。

二、每年由於無法忍受學習壓力而自殺的學生人數逐年增加。去年南京市有一名 14 歲的學生從六樓跳下身亡。在桌子上他留給父母一封遺書，信上說：「爸、媽，我對不起你們，我不是你們的好兒子，我辜負了你們的期望，不管我怎樣努力，絕對考不上南京大學。我要走了，我再也不用忍受學習的壓力了……」

三、那些在學校裡跟不上的學生，挫敗感很大。他們曠課，不學習，而做些偷盜、打架等不法事情。更讓人擔心的是，女孩子和 15 歲以下的少年也開始犯罪了。少年犯罪率逐年上升，這個現象使全社會感到不安。

從 1990 年代起，中國的教育部對教育制度進行了改革，但問題並沒有得到根本的解決。看來中國的教育改革還有很長的路要走。

Lesson 15   How to Handle Criticism

The surgeon reached over and jerked the syringe out of the nurse's hand. "Jane, that's the sloppiest injection I've ever seen!" he snapped. Quickly, his fingers found the vein she had been searching for. Cheeks burning, Jane turned away. Ten years later, Jane's voice still trembles when she relates the experience.

Some of our male co-workers have it easier. They grew up encouraged to play team sports, and they had to handle a coach's yells when they dropped the ball. Now they can see that a goof on the job is like dropping the ball in football; the fumble is embarrassing, but you take it in stride and go on.

But for most women, the path to success was different. As girls, we grew up wanting to be popular; we were praised for what we were, not for what we did. So our reaction to criticism is often, "Someone doesn't like me. I failed to please. I'm a failure."

"I get defensive," says Rhonda, a teacher, "When someone criticizes me, suddenly I'm a little girl again, being scolded, and I want to make excuses. I want to explain that it's not my fault—it's someone else's, or I want to hide and cry."

This kind of response is not constructive; in fact, we should listen. But we also must see criticism for what it is—and isn't.

TAKE A STEP BACK

The first step in handling criticism is to separate yourself from your work.

Deborah writes an in-house newsletter. "I used to feel awful whenever I was asked to rewrite copy," she says. "Every word seemed like a part of me. The real problem was that I was new and not very confident."

As Deborah gained experience, she was able to distance herself from her work. She came to realize that a crossed-out word did not mean someone was crossing her out.

TAKE TIME OUT TO THINK

Learning to distinguish between you and your job does take conscious effort. It always helps to buy a little time for yourself. When a boss or co-worker is critical and you feel the familiar fears or defensive anger well up, take a deep breath, and as soon as possible get off by yourself to examine what was said.

Ask yourself first: is the criticism valid? "Maybe someone objects to what you're doing," says Laura, "not because it's wrong, but simply because it's different or because they don't understand what you want to accomplish. Maybe they aren't aware of all the circumstances."

TAKE THE BULL BY THE HORNS

After cooling off, you can devise a plan that allows you to respond as a rational adult, not a hurt child. You may suggest a conference in which you ask for more information or calmly explain the reasons for your actions or point of view. Or maybe the cooling-off period will simply help you see that you've got to go along with your boss on this one.

Of course, there are times when you shouldn't just go along. Jeannie's former boss used her as a verbal punching bag. "He took out on me all the anger and hostility he felt toward the world," she says. "It was months before I realized that his complaints had nothing to do with the quality of my work. That's when I quit."

TAKE THE BLAME AND GO ON TO OTHER THINGS

When a mistake is real, the best response is to admit it. But as one office friend advises, "Don't mop the floor with your tears." Over-apologizing is as debilitating as extreme defensiveness and is guaranteed to make the other person uncomfortable.

"I couldn't get over it," sputtered a banker about a secretary she had had to replace. "If I pointed out one misspelled word, Sarah spent fifteen minutes telling me how terrible she was, how she would never let it happen again, and please, would I ever forgive her? All I wanted her to do was fix it!"

TAKE THAT CHIP OFF YOUR SHOULDER

Self-criticism can be a way of warding off criticism from others. After all, if we put ourselves down first, who will be mean enough to add to the attack? But this attitude is self-defeating when it discourages us from going after something new.

Truly successful people are those who are proud of their work and are willing to take risks. Usually, they are their own toughest—but often best—critics.

TAKE A TACTFUL APPROACH

How about giving criticism? The old "I-want-to-be-liked" syndrome can make it as hard to give criticism as to take it. Karen thinks she's found the answer.

"Two weeks after I was promoted to first-line supervisor," she remembers, "I had to tell a friend that she was in trouble for not turning in her weekly reports on time. My boss suggested that I tell Judy I didn't want to fix the blame—I just wanted to fix the problem.

That was wonderful advice. It allowed me to state the problem objectively to Judy and she offered the solution."

Criticism in the workplace, whether you're giving it or getting it, is always more effective when you focus on the task rather than on the person. Fixing the problem, not the blame, means that nobody has to feel chewed up. We can still feel whole and learn something in the process.

(893 words)

 Useful Phrases and Expressions

1. the sloppiest injection I've ever seen

2. Jane turned away.

3. She relates the experience.

4. They grew up encouraged to do sth. / We grew up wanting to do sth..

5. handle a coach's yells

6. You take it in stride and go on.

7. We were praised for what we were, not for what we did.

8. I get defensive.

9. This kind of response is not constructive.

10. take a step back

11. separate yourself from your work/distance yourself from your work

12. The real problem is that…

13. gain experience

14. A boss is critical.

15. It always helps to buy a little time for yourself.

16. take conscious effort

17. get off by yourself

18. Is the criticism valid?

19. They aren't aware of all the circumstances.

20. cool off

21. go along with your boss

22. He took out on me all the anger and hostility he felt towards the world.

23. It was months before...

24. have nothing to do with the quality of my work

25. when a mistake is real

26. is guaranteed to (do sth.) make the other person uncomfortable

27. I couldn't get over it.

28. fix the problem/fix the blame

29. Self-criticism can be a way of warding off criticism from others.

30. This attitude is self-defeating.

31. first-line supervisor

32. focus on the task rather than on the person

33. feel chewed out

34. learn sth. in the process

Exercises

I .Comprehension Questions

1. Do you think it is more difficult for women to handle criticism? Why?

2. What is women's reaction to criticism?

3. Is it constructive?

4. Is there a sensible way to handle criticism?

5. What do you do first?

6. After that what do you do?

7. Why do you want to buy yourself a little time?

8. After cooling off what should you do?

9. What is the best response when a mistake is real?

10. What should you avoid?

11. What is so good about self-criticism?

12. Who often are their best critics?

13. And then is it hard to give criticism?

14. How do you do it?

15. Why is it best to fix the problem, not the blame?

16. What is the benefit of doing that?

II .Essay Writing

Write an essay by putting together the answers to the questions in Exercise I, using such joining words as because, and, but and so on.

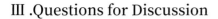

III .Questions for Discussion

1. Do we need criticism? Give examples.

2. Why is it not easy for most people to take criticism? Give examples.

3. What do you think of this text? Give your reasons.

IV .Translation

Put the following Chinese into English, using as many as possible the phrases and expressions you have learned.

　　上星期我的一個同事心臟病突然發作去世了，享年 61 歲。去世前好幾個星期他的心情一直很壞，讓他不痛快的原因是，一個每年一次的學術研討會沒有請他去參加。他在六個月前剛退休，退休前每年他都應邀出席這個研討會，有時還發言。特別使他惱火的是不請他出席既無通知也無任何解釋。他感到自己被冷落了，受到了傷害。他的夫人和朋友勸他冷靜、不要發火。他不聽，而是離他們而去。每天他不出門，把自己關在屋裡，動不動就發火。他的夫人和女兒常常是他的出氣筒。上週五他在電話裡同對方嚷嚷時過於激動死了。他的真正毛病是把名利看得太重，是名利害死了他。辦公室的人都瞭解他，他是一個特別看重得失的人，做錯了事他從不認帳，他永遠是對的。有人要是指出他的錯誤時，他總是為自己辯解，真正出了錯他從不責怪自己而總是責怪他人。他的夫人說自從他當了辦公室主任後一直是這樣，實際上是他害死了自己。

　　說到這裡，我再講一件真事。葛杰今年 88 歲，是一位大學退休數學老師。有一天在校醫院檢查身體時得知自己得了高血壓和心臟病。那時他才 40 歲，不久他知道他的病是遺傳的。不像其他人，他並不驚慌，好像什麼事都沒發生一樣，照樣上課。他十分理智地對待他的健康問題，遇到任何事他都不著急、不生氣。他把什麼事都看得很輕，教研室的老師都因為很喜歡他。他的學生很尊敬他，不僅僅是因為他嚴格、博學而且教得好，還因為他為人善良，樂於助人。他任教 35 年，但退休時只是個副教授，這對他來說無所謂。

他說，他不願為了評個正教授把自己的命也搭進去，只要學生接受他，他就心滿意足了。

退休後他繼續教書，他在家附近的一所中學裡教數學一直到 75 歲。他這樣做並不是為了錢而是想為教育盡份力。他告訴朋友他的長壽祕訣是，不要去追求名利，而是做自己喜歡做的事。

▌Lesson 16　Students Urged to Play Their Part

Hong Kong people have a growing feeling of identity with and responsibility for the environment, Mr. David Chen, the head of the New Territories said at Baptist College yesterday. Speaking at the graduation ceremony, he said that over the past decade attempts have been made to eradicate some of Hong Kong's worst problems: dirt, crime, corruption and drug abuse. The government has tried to explain itself to the people and to make itself more accessible and become involved at the local level. Much more use has been made of advisory boards and committees on such things as social welfare, education and medical services and a public housing authority with responsibility for a vast housing program has been appointed.

"We have established clear policy objectives in a great number of matters which affect the daily lives of the people and people themselves have become involved in these activities through mutual aid and area committees and through district advisory boards," Mr.Chen said.

"It is my belief that these many factors have begun to knit the community together and to build up more coherent and integrated relationships between its various elements, facing our problems together, developing our own particular popular solutions to them and creating a fuller and richer life for our people." He told the students attending the ceremony that they were fortunate to be members of this academic community. They have a greater responsibility than others because with their trained minds, they must be able to per ceive where Hong Kong is weak and where its strengths lie. "You have the vision to see the need to participate and to respond sensibly to the weaknesses of our society." He listed corruption, dirt, crime, carelessness, discourtesy and unconcern as some of the symptoms of a divided society.

"You cannot afford to stand aside secure in the small world of family and friends because, if you do, we will be overwhelmed by the negative forces which are ever-present inside our society and we will be unable to face the undoubted challenges that lie ahead."

On community development he refused to accept the proposition that the people of Hong Kong could not develop a common sense of purpose to build a healthy and happy society, that they could not have a pride in the place and its achievements, that they could not develop a real sense of responsibility for the environment and the conduct of the people. At the end of his speech he said, "We are just as capable of working out our own Hong Kong solutions to life in the world of today, and we look to people such as yourselves to come forward with ideas and to participate in the search for these solutions."

(456 words)

 Useful Phrases and Expressions

1. have a growing feeling of

2. Attempts have been made to do sth.

3. eradicate problems

4. The government has tried to explain itself to the people.

5. make itself more accessible

6. become involved at the local level

7. advisory boards and committees

8. A public housing authority has been appointed.

9. a vast housing program

10. We have established clear policy objectives in a great number of matters.

11. It is my belief that...

12. knit the community together

13. build up coherent and integrated relationships between...

14. develop our own particular popular solutions to the problems

15. create a fuller and richer life for our people

16. with their trained minds

17. face our problems together

18. respond sensibly to the weaknesses of our society

19. a divided society

20. We will be overwhelmed by the negative forces.

21. have a pride in

22. be capable of doing something

23. work out our own Hong Kong solutions to life in the world of today

24. We look to people such as yourselves.

25. to come forward with ideas

26. in the search for

 Exercises

I .Comprehension Questions

1. Who is Mr.David Chen?

2. Where was he yesterday? What was he there for?

3. What did he say about Hong Kong people today?

4. What are the worst problems in Hong Kong?

5. Has the government done anything to eradicate the problems?

6. What did he say about Hong Kong society?

7. What has the government done to knit the society together?

8. Why did he want to tell the students about the Hong Kong society, its problems and the efforts the government has been making to create a better Hong Kong?

9. What did he want the students to do?

10. How did he convince the students that they have a responsibility in building a healthy and happy society?

11. What do you think of Mr. David Chen's speech? Do you think he is a good speaker? Why?

II .Essay Writing

Write an essay by putting together the answers to the questions in Exercise I, using such joining words as because, and, but and so on.

III .Questions for Discussion

1. What problems do we have in the mainland?

2. What are the root causes of these problems?

3. Do you think you have a responsibility to join the efforts to eradicate these problems? How?

4. Is it difficult for the government to build a fuller and richer life for the people? What are the difficulties?

IV .Translation

Put the following Chinese into English, using as many as possible the phrases and expressions you have learned.

在過去的十幾年裡，儘管中國政府在盡力去縮小貧富之間的差距，但這個差距還是變得越來越大。有關部門在一些主要城鎮的 5.4 萬戶中做了一項調查，發現 10% 的人占有 45% 的城市財富。上海一座價值 1.3 億人民幣的高級住宅大樓被一位 35 歲的男士購買，然而在西北一個所謂富裕地區卻有 19 萬人只能勉強維持生活。在北京一位 26 歲的年輕人買下了一輛價值 92 萬美元的賽車，可是在某些貧困農村，農民從未見過 100 元人民幣的鈔票。在南京有些還不算最富的人一個月的工資是 10 萬元人民幣，然而一些無業者只能靠每月 100 多元的補助來餬口。這種貧富差距的例子不勝枚舉。

造成這個問題的原因十分複雜。中國正在經歷一場漫長的經濟轉型。貧富差距問題不僅僅存在於中國，這個問題在西方已存在了近一個世紀。實際上它是一個全球性問題。但這並不能給我們一個理由讓這個問題繼續存在下去並變得更為嚴重。為了使這個問題有所緩解，政府對農村已制定了明確的政策性目標。一系列關係到增加農民收入和改善他們日常生活的措施已在全國落實。針對失業人員，政府也採取了一些特殊的辦法來幫助他們。形勢在好轉，我們相信在今後幾年內，貧富差距在中國會有所縮小。

Lesson 17   Village Thinks Small and Shines

The little village of Khandia has shown that India could save millions of dollars in its campaign to provide energy to remote areas. To date, says Dr.Amin, emphasis has been on large-scale energy projects that require heavy investment in mining, transportation and other development costs. Khandia, he argues, has shown that modest local schemes are just as efficient and much cheaper.

Dr.Amin is head of the Gujarat Energy Development Agency (GEDA). The agency was founded to help villages establish noncommercial sources of energy. It took its mandate a step further, creating an integrated system designed to provide all a village's energy by using a combination of small-scale collection methods. Dr.Amin, an industrialist and electrical engineer says, "Here is a case study of decentralization to be closely examined. Here production, utilization of energy based on locally available renewable resources of energy are in the hands of the village community itself and not in the hands of government. If the villagers of Khandia succeed, this experiment can change the face of India."

A village of about 1000 people, Khandia was chosen for Amin's experiment because "it had as many hostile conditions as one could think of." If they could be overcome, then similar rural energy centres could be established anywhere in India. Khandia is typical of thousands of Gujarat villages. About 45 kilometres south of Baroda, it is far from the nearest tarmac road, and seldom visited by doctors, social workers, agricultural experts or forest officials. Its nearest primary health center, when the experiment started three years ago, was eight kilometers away. The village's poorly irrigated, largely infertile 186 hectares of agricultural land provided poor crops of rice, wheat, millet and cotton. The women cooked on open hearths after scrabbling for firewood and collecting cow dung. Most villagers suffered from lung trouble. There was little work available and superstition was rife among its poor, ill-educated population. There was little that Khandia had going for it, except the Gujarat Energy Development Agency. Rather than rely on the costly energy supplies that have resulted from India's massive investments in industrial-level production, Amin and his team decided to look for alternative sources.

GEDA persuaded the 130 families in Khandia to form an energy co-operative. They were to share all energy generated and to generate it themselves. First, 12 hectares of wasteland were planted with fast-growing trees like eucalyptus and tamarind. The 255 tons of wood from this energy plantation, plus waste materials, will create gas for an engine that, in turn, will power a generator. The generator will produce 25 kilowatts of power for street-lighting, two light points in each house, pumps for the community water supply, the flour mill, and local small industries. Four smaller gas-run pumps will draw water and distribute it through irrigation channels to 70 hectares of farmland.

As a second source of energy, GEDA installed an 85-cubic-metre community biogas plant. Each villager using it will sell the plant three baskets of animal waste or agricultural waste daily to keep it operating. The plant will supply gas for an hour at a time, twice a day, to cooking gas connections and stoves now installed in every house.

The third source of energy being tapped is the sun. Khandia can now have its own public health center. The center has a refrigerator run on photovoltaic cells, a 250-litre solar hot water system and a solar still for distilled water. The village also now boasts a community center with solar-powered television and radio sets.

Providing this total energy to Khandia has cost only Rs (Rupees) 1875 ($150) considerably less than conventional power sources would have cost. Amin comments, "if only one-quarter of one percent of the power sector allocation were set aside for further experiments, a thousand model villages could be established. Thousands of others would soon follow their example and India's villages would no longer have to face the major problem of energy poverty."

(658 words)

 Useful Phrases and Expressions

1. remote areas

2. to date

3. Emphasis has been on large-scale energy projects.

4. heavy or massive investment in

5. Modest local schemes are just as efficient and much cheaper.

6. non-commercial sources of energy

7. take a step further

8. an integrated system

9. small or large scale

10. a case study of decentralization

11. renewable resources of energy

12. Something is in the hands of somebody.

13. change the face of

14. be chosen for

15. as many hostile conditions as one could think of

16. It is seldom visited by doctors.

17. health center

18. poorly irrigated, infertile land

19. poor crops of rice, wheat, millet and cotton

20. cow dung

21. There was little work available.

22. ill-educated population

23. There was little that Khandia had going for it.

24. industrial level production

25. look for alternative sources

26. an energy co-operative

27. 2 fast-growing trees

28. irrigation channels

29. biogas plant

30. animal, agricultural waste

31. keep it operating

32. be set aside for further experiments

33. model villages

34. energy poverty

 Exercises

I .Comprehension Questions

1. What has the little village of Khandia shown?

2. Who started this energy project? What was GEDA's job?

3. Why did Dr.Amin and his team choose Khandia for their experiment?

4. How did they go about their experiment in Khandia?

5. What is the significance of Dr.Amin's experiment?

II .Essay Writing

Write an essay by putting together the answers to the questions in Exercise I, using such joining words as because, and, but and so on.

III .Questions for Discussion

1. What does Dr.Amin and his team's experiment tell people?

2. Would you say Dr.Amin's experiment is highly significant for most developing countries? Give your reasons.

IV .Translation

Put the following Chinese into English, using as many as possible the phrases and expressions you have learned.

在新加坡你可以見到各種膚色的人。新加坡是一個多元文化、多種族的國家，但人們卻能和平相處，各民族之間的關係十分和諧融洽。是什麼因素使整個社會能緊緊結合在一起呢？兩個字：教育。從 1980 年代起，新加坡政府花大力氣來提高教育質量。他們堅信只有透過教育才能使整個社會緊密地結合在一起。

新加坡是一個小島國，面積只有 600 多平方公里，自然資源貧乏。在這種情況下，人力資源成為最重要的資源。因此，每年在教育上政府投入了大量的資金，總額占全國財政收入的 5% ～ 6 ％。這個比例大大高於亞洲其他國家對教育的投入。所有的學校都享受政府財政補貼。

新加坡教育的核心是培養公民的責任感和誠信意識。透過教育,政府意在構建一個高素質的社會。從小學到大學,學生都受到東西文化的薰陶。學生都必須學習雙語——英語和漢語,並要把它們學好。有些學校除了漢語課外其他的課程都用英語教授。學生可以在學習西方先進科技的同時學習東方傳統道德規範和價值觀。

　　雖然不是每個人都能上大學,但每人都有接受較好教育的機會,機會對每個人來說都是平等的。人們清楚地知道,受教育不只是為了拿學位和證書,也是為了獲取一個發展自己能力的機會。只要一個人誠信、努力,他一定會過上好日子。

Lesson 18   You Can Speak in Public

It's a most valuable skill, for those who do it successfully to reap substantial rewards. Here's a guide to the essentials. When someone asks you to deliver a talk in front of a group, what's your reaction? If you're like most people, it's sheer terror. The No.1 phobia in America is the fear of public speaking, according to a survey. Their problem, generally, is in talking to groups of five or ten people. A business executive, a supervisor in a factory, a sectionworker in an office all can increase their effectiveness through BETTER PUBLIC SPEAKING. The opportunities are limitless.

Can you improve your speaking skill? Of course! Anyone can. All you have to do is learn how. The two steps in making any speech— preparation and delivery—are equally important. Here are four rules for planning your talk:

1. Pick the right subject. It should be a topic about which you have strong feelings. The only way to be comfortable in front of an audience is to know what you're talking about, and to believe in what you're trying to get across. While the American hostages were being held in Iraq, many of their wives appeared on national television. Even without formal training, these women spoke with true eloquence. Their pleas came from the heart. Choose a subject of direct interest to your listeners and get the message across to them. Assume that you've come up with an idea to improve office efficiency. If you're called upon to sell your proposal to the board of directors, emphasize the profits it will bring; when presenting the plan to the people who will implement it, stress how it will make their jobs easier. Everyone wants to know: What's in it for me?

2. Organize your points logically. You need a beginning—usually a brief description of the problem you intend to attack; a middle that enumerates the main points in your solution; and an end that summarizes your entire presentation. An old rule for speakers puts it this way: "tell them what you're going to tell them; then tell them; and finally, tell them what you've told them."

3. Rehearse in private. After you've planned your presentation you need to practice delivering it. It's best to do this in private, not in front of a friend or spouse. You are rehearsing a speech to a group, not a one-to-one discussion. Try to visualize the audience. "See and hear" the positive responses you'll be receiving. Whenever possible, do a final review in the room where you'll be speaking. This way, you will feel at home during your actual performance.

4. Keep notes to a minimum. The worst thing to do is try to read your speech. It's virtually impossible to make a reading sound spontaneous. If necessary, list your major headings on index cards—with only a few words on each card. A quick glance will trigger your thoughts. The less you refer to notes, the better you'll communicate with your audience. Public speaking is essentially a matter of communication between you and your audience. For most speakers, copious notes are more of a hindrance than a help.

But no matter how well you prepare, you also have to deliver the speech. Here are three rules for your delivery:

1. Make friends with your audience. There's no need for oratory in the old-fashioned sense. Be yourself, and you'll seldom go wrong. Simple words and short sentences are best. Examples and anecdotes also help to build a bridge to your listeners. Also, be sure to look at the audience and maintain eye contact. Seek out the friendly faces. Ignore any that are not. For the platform pro, humor

is a requirement, but for the average person, it is not necessary unless it makes a point and unless you use it well.

2. Never apologize. If you feel any shortcomings, ignore them. If you have a cold, don't mention it. To be confident, act confident. If you happen to forget what you are going to say next, keep it to yourself. Your listeners won't know unless you tell them. Instead, repeat your last point to give yourself a breather. Or go on to something else. Your audience wants you to do well. Why disappoint it. If you suffer from stage fright, don't worry about it. A certain degree of tension is helpful. I often tell my clients, "We won't remove your butterflies entirely; we'll just get them to fly in formation!"

3. Build to a climax. There should be a compelling purpose to your talk. Aim toward it throughout your speech. Then close with a call to action. Don't wait too long to finish. Be sure that you stop speaking before the audience stops listening. George M.Cohan had the right idea: "Always leave them wanting more." The old saying, "practice makes perfect," applies in public speaking too. So speak at every opportunity. The rewards can be enormous. Indeed, with practice, you can use speaking as a springboard to success and a fuller, more satisfying life.

(830 words)

 Useful Phrases and Expressions

1. valuable skill for somebody to do something

2. Here's a guide to the essentials.

3. deliver a talk in front of

4. What's your reaction?

5. Their problem, generally, is in...

6. increase the effectiveness through...

7. The opportunities are limitless.

8. All you have to do is...

9. The two steps are equally important.

10. have strong feelings about something

11. be comfortable in front of an audience

12. get the message across to people

13. formal training

14. speak with true eloquence

15. Their pleas come from the heart.

16. You've come up with an idea to improve office efficiency.

17. a brief description of the problem you intend to attack

18. rehearse in private

19. one-to-one discussion

20. positive responses

21. feel at home

22. keep notes to a minimum

23. The worst thing to do is...

24. It's virtually impossible to do something.

25. A quick glance will trigger your thoughts.

26. be yourself

27. You'll seldom go wrong.

28. the platform pro

29. It makes a point.

30. give yourself a breather

31. stage fright

32. butterflies in the stomach

33. get them to fly information

34. There should be a compelling purpose to your talk.

35. the rewards can be enormous

36. springboard to success

37. a fuller and more satisfying life

 Exercises

I .Comprehension Questions

1. What is the writer's answer when asked whether you can improve your speaking skill?

2. How can you do that?

3. How many steps are there in making a speech?

4. Are there any rules to help you prepare a speech? How many are there?

5. Please explain them one by one in a simple and concise way.

6. What are the rules of delivering a speech?

7. Please explain them one by one in a concise way.

II .Essay Writing

Write an essay by putting together the answers to the questions in Exercise I, using such joining words as because, and, but and so on.

III .Questions for Discussion

1. Why is it that it is a most valuable skill for a person to learn to make a good speech in the world today?

2. Have you discovered that some of the rules of making good speeches will also help you with your English studies? What are they?

IV .Translation

Put the following Chinese into English, using as many as possible the phrases and expressions you have learned.

韓偉擁有全國最大的蛋雞場（laying hen farm），全世界最大的鮑魚（abalone）養殖場。「咯咯噠」蛋是他蛋場的品牌產品，被國家評為優質蛋。日本允許「咯咯噠」蛋進入它的市場。2000 年 7 月，韓偉被世界蛋品協會吸納為唯一能代表中國的會員。他的蛋場年產雞蛋 5000 萬公斤左右。他是中國最大的蛋王，進入了富比士（Forbes）名單。

韓偉出生在一個貧寒的農民家庭，幼年時隨父母從老家瀋陽移居大連。剛到一個新城市時，全家的生活十分艱難。他們沒有正式的工作，只能靠撿垃圾和掏大糞（nightsoil）來餬口。1982 年一次偶然的機會，他聽人說美國的蛋雞產蛋量比本地雞產蛋量高四倍。經過三天認真考慮，他決定做蛋品生意。他從親戚朋友那裡借了 3000 元，買了 50 隻美國蛋雞。沒想到一舉成功。不到兩年的時間，他的蛋雞場從 50 隻發展到 8000 隻。1984 年，他得到銀行 15 萬的貸款，辦了一個大雞場。

可是好景不長，麻煩來了。他的蛋雞一隻一隻地死。由於他從未受過正式培訓，不知道怎麼辦。但他清楚地知道不能讓這種情況繼續下去，一定得想個法子。兩天兩夜的冥思苦想，他想出了個主意。讓他的妻子馬上去北京學習如何治雞病。同時，他自己剖剪死雞，想找出雞死的原因。經過幾星期的艱苦工作，他最終找出了原因。妻子一從北京回來，他倆就地把雞場搬到一座山頭上，在那裡雞可以養得更好。新的雞場很大，是一個工業化的養雞場。雞場還有種雞場（stud chicken farm）、飼料廠和一個中型獸藥廠（drug factory for live stock）。韓偉的目標是在時機成熟時，在北京建造一個綜合生態場（comprehensive eco-farm）。

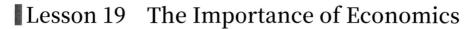

Lesson 19　The Importance of Economics

Economics is a way of understanding human behavior and of solving problems that characteristically involve scarcity. Economics is important because it provides a method to help clarify a wide range of problems affecting human welfare. It has traditionally been thought that economics is concerned with such broad topics as wealth and income; the production and distribution of goods; money and banking;the determination of prices; employment and unemployment; shortterm changes in the level of business activity; and long-term trends that make some nations rich and keep others poor. But economics has actually been concerned also with the welfare, working and living conditions, and freedom of the individual person. The nineteenthcentury English economist Alfred Marshall sought to show the universal significance of economics when he said that it is a study of mankind in the ordinary business of life. He also noted that economics examines that part of individual social activity that is concerned with getting and using the materials necessary for health and happiness.

Economics is a study of wealth and an important part of the study of man. This is because man's character has been shaped by his daily work, and the material resources he gains from it. In general, then, economics is about individual and social behavior and values. You cannot understand much about your society without having some knowledge of economics.

THE IMPORTANCE OF ECONOMICS TO THE INDIVIDUAL

What are an individual's goals in life? Perhaps none of us would answer the question in exactly the same way; a person's specific goals and wants are unique. Yet given his goals in life, a person wants enough income to enable him to live as he chooses. This is true in both rich and poor countries. An adequate income is essential if men are to achieve a sense of personal dignity, psychological security, and a life with many moral values, rather than a life that is miserable, limited and base.

Economic factors affect the lives of all men, not just the poor. They affect the major personal decisions that a person makes about what career to choose, where to live, etc. Economic considerations also influence a multitude of small daily decisions that all people must make; for instance, what a person eats, whether he walks or rides to town, and many other decisions that constitute a substantial part of the way a person lives, exercises his taste and judgment and achieves personal goals.

Naturally, economic considerations, in the narrow sense of monetary gains or losses, are not the only factors that influence personal decisions. A person's talents, tastes, social attitudes, psychological constitution, values, and aspirations also affect the choices he makes, including economic choices. However, there is plenty of evidence that economic factors are extensive and potent in affecting personal choices and decisions.

The individual is also affected by economic events that lie beyond his personal control. If his nation enters a period of rapidly rising prices, the value of his cash, and his savings account at the bank, if he has one, will diminish. If his nation is forced to reduce its imports from other countries because it is not exporting enough goods, the individual may find that he must pay more for domestically produced substitutes or possibly proceed without some goods entirely.

THE IMPORTANCE OF ECONOMICS TO BUSINESS

Much business activity consists of collecting economic information and making estimates and decisions based on that information. Usually, a businessman's goal is to make a profit. In pursuit of that goat, he must seek to determine what the market for his products is and will be, whether he should maintain his prices, increase or reduce them, increase or reduce his advertising expenditures, and add to or reduce his sales staff. He must seek to reduce his costs of doing business to meet the pressure of competition from other business. He must decide whether to buy new machinery to increase the productivity of his plant. He must seek to substitute less expensive materials for more expensive ones. He must try to employ workers who will produce enough at a low-enough cost to allow his business to make a profit. The businessman must be alert to new industrial developments that may create new opportunities for him, and when such developments arise, he must decide whether to switch to different types of production or to try to develop new products through research. He must determine whether he has enough productive capacity to meet the demand for his products, whether he has sufficient distribution established for getting his goods to possible buyers. The businessman also must study his financial situation continuously.

Determining the answers to all these questions involves collecting information, analyzing economic and financial data, making rational business decisions, and applying business instincts or feelings about the prospects of particular actions. The businessman lives in a world that cannot be perfectly measured and he must have the courage to rely on his instincts. But clear economic information and analysis can undoubtedly help him make better business decisions and reduce the amount of uncertainty that he faces, and thus help his business prosper rather than fall.

THE IMPORTANCE OF ECONOMICS TO NATIONS

As with individuals and businesses, economic factors also seriously affect the ability of nations to deal with their domestic and international problems and therefore their growth or decline. Throughout history, economic progress has contributed to the rise of great powers, and economic failures have contributed to their decline and fall. Nor can recent political history be understood without comprehending the importance of economic events. One of the major political issues of our time is the condition of the materially poor nations of the world. They are determined to end their poverty and the same time to achieve national political independence.

To deal with the present international situation and the drive of the poor countries for economic and political development, the oldest and most basic question of economics must be answered. What makes a nation wealthy? Another important concept must also be considered—the freedom of the individual. The basic problem is not simply how to increase economic wealth, but rather how to increase it while preserving individual freedom.

(1026 words)

 Useful Phrases and Expressions

1. a method to help clarify a wide range of problems

2. human welfare

3. It has traditionally been thought that...

4. distribution of goods

5. short-term changes in

6. long-term trends

7. Economics has actually been concerned with...

8. the universal significance of

9. Man's character has been shaped by his daily work and the material resources he gains.

10. cannot understand much about... without

11. goals in life

12. live as he chooses

13. Economic factors affect the lives of all men.

14. Economic considerations also influence a multitude of small daily decisions.

15. in the narrow/broad sense

16. psychological constitution

17. There is plenty of evidence that...

18. beyond one's control

19. rapidly rising prices

20. proceed without some goods entirely

21. make estimates

22. advertising expenditures

23. meet the pressure of

24. increase the productivity of the plant

25. substitute less expensive materials for more expensive ones

26. When such developments arise, he must decide whether to switch to...

27. productive capacity

28. possible buyers

29. make rational business decisions

30. apply business instincts or feelings about

31. rely on his instincts

32. growth and decline

33. end their poverty

 Exercises

I .Comprehension Questions

1. What is economics?

2. What has economics actually been concerned with?

3. Why is economics a study of wealth and an important part of study of man?

4. Is economics important to the individual? Why and how does the writer explain his point?

5. Why does the writer say economics is important to business? What are the facts that the writer uses to explain his conclusion?

6. Finally, how does the writer explain to the readers that economics is important to nations?

II .Essay Writing

Write an essay by putting together the answers to the questions in Exercise I, using such joining words as because, and, but and so on.

III .Questions for Discussion

1. What is economics and what does it deal with?

2. Do you think it is extremely important to a country? Give some specific examples.

3. Do you think everybody should have some knowledge of economics? Why?

IV .Translation

Put the following Chinese into English, using as many as possible the phrases and expressions you have learned.

提到丁學金這個名字，絕大多數上海人可能想不起他是誰（doesn't ring a bell）。他是慈愛醫院的院長。慈愛醫院是上海第一家民營慈善醫院。丁學金投入了他的全部家產創辦了這家醫院。和其他新醫院不同，在開業那天，他沒有舉行任何隆重的開業典禮，這麼做的主要原因是他不想借用媒體為他的醫院做宣傳。在那天，他和醫院醫生辦了一次義診，為那些付不起醫療費的人看病。他篤信從病人口中人們會瞭解他的醫院。當人們問他辦此醫院的宗旨時，他說要讓更多的人知道紅十字會的博愛精神，並要把這種精神推廣到全中國。

丁學金本人是一名腫瘤專家。他說窮人也應享受好的醫療保障，這個權利不應被剝奪。迄今為止，全中國還有相當多的人由於經濟條件的限制，病了不能及時就醫。政府和社會有義務照顧這些窮人的健康（physical well-being），然而由於多種原因很難做到。對醫務人員來說，見到病人僅僅是因為沒錢而死去是件十分痛心的事。他和其他醫生作為社會成員有責任和義務幫助窮人，特別是那些失業者和孤寡老人。

但醫院一開始就不順，最大的問題是資金。他的醫院不享受國家補貼，加上得不到社會在經濟方面的支援，資金問題就變得更為嚴重了。而且他的醫院不在政府醫療保險定點醫院名列之中，病人就不去他的醫院看病了，因此，醫院無法透過正常盈利來維持運轉。如果這種情況繼續下去，你說會有奇蹟出現嗎？丁學金也在開業當年病逝在自己創立的醫院。

Lesson 20   Why Japanese Cars Still Sell

Why do Japanese cars sell so well? They are by no means perfect. Insist Fortune magazine, "in comfort, quiet, corrosion resistance, and reliability of engine and transmission, American cars can claim the advantage." They may also be safer. Two years ago, all Japanese entries failed National Highway Traffic Safety Administration crash-barrier tests. Insurance claims for inj uries in U.S. autoaccidents are most frequent for Japanese-made cars. But Japanese cars seem the ideal way to cut fuel costs. Because Japan has virtually no domestic oil resources, its gas is twice as expensive as U.S. gas and fuel-stingy cars have long been a must for the Japanese.

PRIDE OF WORKMANSHIP

Fuel efficiency, however, is not the only quality that attracts buyers to Japanese cars, says a Tokyo-based U.S. management consultant, "whether justified or not, the feeling of many Americans is that the new car's value-for-money and subsequent maintenance costs make many Japanese designs the better buy." Astonishingly, U.S. automotive engineers appear to agree. In a recent poll by the respected trade journal WARD'S AUTO WORLD, 47.2 percent of those who design and build cars for five American auto companies said the best quality cars were now coming from Japan. Only 27.2 percent voted for their own makes. Summarizing the poll, the magazine commented, "Japanese superiority stems from better workmanship, attention to fine detail, and rapport with management that lets assembly-line voices be heard." As General Motors' Lee Caudill, Fisher Body Division senior engineer, puts it, "In Japan, quality and pride of workmanship are a way of life."

An understanding of the basis of the Japanese auto industry begins with the country's centuries-old system of Taue, irrigated rice growing. Construction and cultivation of small, water filled paddies have historically required close cooperation. A brief harvesting season also taught people to work hard at jobs assigned to them by group leaders. An old saying epitomizes the frenetic nature of farming in feudal Japan: "One day's delay means one month's evil fortune."

GROUP LOYALTY

The Japanese auto company is a direct descendant of this campaign-style agriculture. There is also the old cultural habit of being part of a Dantai—a group of institution. Through American auto workers, group loyalty usually translates into allegiance to their trade union—the powerful United Auto Workers. But in Japan, where Occupation Supreme Commander Gen. Douglas Macarthur ordered the establishment of unions, the Japanese formed them around the enterprise or plant in which they worked. In most instances these enterprise unions made for close contact and mutual understanding between managers and union leaders. The Japanese car's value-formoney reputation derives at least in part from this.

When sales fall in the United States, car firms lay off workers. But Japanese auto makers often undertake seemingly irrelevant diversifications, so employees remain productive in slack periods. Nissan makes textile machinery. A Honda subsidiary makes thermos jugs and athletic equipment. Toyota sells prefabricated houses.

Such consideration pays off in worker loyalty. The formerly debt-plagued Toyo Kogyo Co. Ltd., producer of Mazda and now Japan's third largest auto maker, offers a remarkable example of what good management-worker relationship can accomplish. In the early 1970s the success of a line of cars powered by the revolutionary Wankel rotary engine encouraged the company to gather in a 37,000 man workforce to produce an anticipated one million vehicles per year. But the October 1973 Arab oil embargo and subsequent fuel price rises eroded the market, especially for Mazda's comparatively gas-thirsty rotaries. Sales dropped drastically. In 1975, the company reported 70 million in losses and 1.5 billion in debt.

COMBAT DUTY

Pledged to cut the payroll only as a last resort, management held meetings to keep workers informed of the company's position. At the main Mazda plant in Hiroshima, production controller Yoshiki Yamasaki introduced production roles that meant extra workloads for many. Mazda instituted a floating system under which men looking after one machine took over three or four. Workers willingly accepted the challenge. If anything, morale seemed higher. The new procedures helped lift Toyo Kogyo productivity from 19.3 vehicles per worker yearly in 1975 to 44.4 in 1980. Toyo Kogyo's most radical step, however, was sending more than 5000 production workers, engineers, designers, assembly-line technicians on a door-knocking sales campaign. "It was like being drafted for special combat duty," recalls Nobutaka Nojinma, a 36-year-old engineer who was given a week of sales training and moved to a bachelor apartment 90 miles from his Hiroshima family. On his first day, he knocked on more than 100 doors without finding a single Mazda prospect. But he didn't think of quitting. After a year of selling he was back in Hiroshima, proud of having found buyers for 42 Mazdas, well over the professional salesmen's average. His head was full of ideas for answering the customers' demands. Today, as a result of his and his co-workers' efforts, Toyo Kogyo is regularly exceeding production sales goals, with 1.2 million cars and trucks annually.

MORE SERVICE, LESS MONEY

Since most Japanese companies reward Dantai loyalty with cradle-to-grave security, Japanese auto workers accept much lower compensation than Americans. Even allowing for bonuses, the average Nissan assembly-line worker earns less than $10 an hour. Similar General Motors' employees get up to $19 an hour, including fringe benefits. The total Japanese cost advantage runs from about $1200 to $1500 per vehicle. In many other ways, Japanese workers give their companies extraordinary service, much of which is passed on to car buyers in value-for-money. Dedication? Fewer than 20 percent of salaried workers use their paid vacation time. More than 10 percent take none. Employees of all Japanese companies work an average 2110 hours a year, compared with 2060 hours a year, including overtime for Americans. Japanese auto workers put in 2230 hours including overtime.

Strikes? Toyota had its last strike in 1950, Nissan in 1953. Since then, Japan's two biggest auto makers have not lost a single hour of production to labour unrest. Absenteeism? At Toyota and Nissan, an average day sees 4 to 7 percent of workers off the job. Comparable figures for some US assembly lines: 17 percent off work.

Yet another factor is the widespread use of robots. At Nissan's showcase plant, outside Tokyo, 6200 workers turn out 37,000 cars a month in one of the world's most automated auto factories. Here rows of futuristic machines bob and weave beside assembly lines, clamping, bending and welding pieces of metal into the shape of a Datsun compact in less than a minute. Ironically, many of the robots that are cutting Japan's auto production costs are adaptations of American designs not yet fully exploited by Detroit.

QUALITY CONTROL

Of all the debts the Japanese auto industry owes to the United States, perhaps the greatest is the idea of quality control (QC), brought to Japan in 1950 by W Edwards Deming, a U.S. statistician and adviser to the Occupation authorities. The concept, based on statistical analysis, marked a turning point for Japanese manufacturers whose search for foreign markets was hampered by low productivity and reputation for shoddy merchandise.

The average compact car consists of about 30,000 separate parts, the failure of any one of which can result in anything from annoyance to disaster. QC aims at building in quality from the design stage. Dantai-happy employee groups record product defects, identify causes, make a striking contribution to productivity. Last year, the 27,000 workers producing Mazda cars submitted more than 900,000 suggestions. And Nissan's QC groups earned the company a potential $30 million in savings.

Now then, do U.S. assembly lines cope with the Japanese challenge? According to Joseph Juran, a U.S. quality-control engineer who has served as a consultant to auto companies worldwide, 80 percent of the defects in the U.S. auto industry are management-controllable. He calls for long-term training, "beginning at the top like the Japanese."

Whatever is to be done, the visitor to Japan's remarkable auto plants is left with the strong impression that it would be wise to do it soon—if the Japanese are not to hold their auto-making lead forever.

As Deming puts it, "The Japanese aren't standing still, waiting around to play tag with us!"

(1350 words)

 ## Useful Phrases and Expressions

1. Japane

2. se cars sell so well.

3. They are by no means perfect.

4. corrosion resistance

5. reliability of engine

6. the ideal way to do sth.

7. fuel-stingy cars

8. fuel efficiency

9. Tokyo-based U.S. management consultant

10. whether justified or not

11. value-for-money

12. Japanese superiority stems from better workmanship.

13. attention to fine detail

14. Let assembly-line voices be heard.

15. Quality and pride of workmanship are a way of life.

16. centuries-old system of

17. close cooperation

18. work hard at jobs assigned to them

19. in most instances

20. these enterprise unions made for close contact between

21. in part

22. sales fall

23. in slack periods

24. Such consideration pays off in worker loyalty.

25. debt-plagued Toyo

26. offer a remarkable example of what good relationship can accomplish

27. erode the market

28. gas-thirsty cars

29. cut the payroll only as a last resort

30. keep workers informed of the company's position

31. institute a floating system

32. lift productivity from... to...

33. radical step

34. His head was full of ideas.

35. reward Dantai loyalty with cradle-to-grave security

36. 4 to 7 percent of workers off the job (off work)

37. shoddy merchandise

38. product defects

39. identify causes

40. The defects are management-controllable.

41. He calls for long-term training.

42. begin at the top

 **Exercises**

I .Comprehension Questions

1. Which cars have more advantages in terms of comfort, quiet, corrosion resistance and reliability of engine and transmission, the Japanese cars or the American cars?

2. What is the advantage that the Japanese cars have?

3. Is fuel efficiency the only quality that attracts buyers to Japanese cars? Is there any other quality that makes Japanese cars sell so well?

4. What makes Japan have such superiority?

5. What was the frenetic nature of farming in feudal Japan?

6. How does this nature of farming influence the Japanese auto industry?

7. What is the thing that knits the Japanese auto company together? Give examples.

8. What is combat duty? How does the company benefit from it?

9. Can you give more examples to show good management-work er relationship?

10. What is the result of this relationship?

11. Besides all the factors that help the Japanese cars sell well, what is another important factor that gives the Japanese cars an advantage?

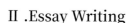

II .Essay Writing

Write an essay by putting together the answers to the questions in Exercise I, using such joining words as because, and, but and so on.

III .Questions for Discussion

1. What do you think are the things that make a company or a factory successful? Why?

2. What impresses you most in the passage? Give your reasons.

3. Does this passage have some practical value for you? What is it?

IV .Translation

Put the following Chinese into English, using as many as possible the phrases and expressions you have learned.

談到問題時，通常人們的反應是問題都是不好的。但如果你仔細想想，就會發現有問題並不是件壞事。我們需要問題。大部分情況下，問題使得我們堅強和聰明。從某種意義上說，人的性格部分是由他經歷的大量的問題塑造而成的。在我們的社會中，問題是永遠都存在的，沒有問題這個世界就沒有生氣了。老問題解決了，新問題就出現了，問題一個一個得到解決，社會就向前發展了。從某種意義上來說，歷史就是這樣形成的。

然而，人在為自己製造問題方面是極為能幹的。很多問題都成了社會問題甚至世界性問題，例如汙染、貧困、吸毒、人口過多、家庭暴力、犯罪及社會老齡化。人們用了大量的人力、物力和財力製造了這些問題。可笑的是，人們用更多的人力、物力和財力來消除這些問題。你不得不想：我們怎麼了？不幸的是在我們國家上述問題都存在，有的問題一年比一年嚴重。這些問題已經嚴重地影響了社會的發展。談到這裡，我以中國的貧富問題為例。這個問題是在 1980 年代末才出現的，而其發展是驚人地快。據初步估計，中國現在還有不少的人生活在貧困線以下，他們的年收入只有 865 元，也就是說他們一個月只能賺 72 元或一天不到 2.5 元。在物價和費用一直上漲的一個社會裡，2.5 元能幹什麼呢？ 2.5 元在一些大城市裡只能買一杯茶。使我感到更辛酸的是,有很多人一天還賺不到 2 元錢。然而在北京、上海或深圳的一些人一天就能賺 1 萬元。他們還不是最富的。在北京一個車展上有一輛車的價格是 900 萬元左右,開展剛一小時就有人買了。在不太富裕的地方的一個普通農民要不吃不喝要 4000 年才能賺到這些錢。可見中國貧富差距是多麼嚴重了。

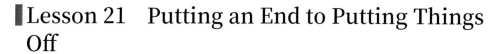

Lesson 21   Putting an End to Putting Things Off

You've filed your nails, confirmed next week's lunch dates, sharpened every pencil in the place. Now, learn to eliminate those time-gobbling tactics and become productive plus!

Practice Telling Time

"I can read War and Peace in two nights." "I'll take a half-day off to find a new apartment." "I can knock off my annual report in an hour." You can probably tell that these expectations are unrealistic. It's obvious that each of these activities will take longer, a whole lot longer, than the time allotted. Yet, to the student who is behind in his Russian literature class, to the hurried school teacher who wants to move out of her parents' house, to the sales manager who hasn't compiled his yearly figure, these estimates seem possible.

One way to counter such wishful thinking is to compare your predictions about how long things take with what actually happens when you do them. Many people assume they do know how long they spend on everyday activities but find that their predictions were way off when they actually take a measurement. One procrastinator, a New York City businessman, planned his drives to Long Island using the timetable "it takes fortyfive minutes without traffic." This is true, but had he ever driven to Long Island without traffic? Not likely.

Learn to Use Little Bits of Time

Alan Lakein made a great suggestion for procrastinators when he described the "Swiss cheese" method of time management in his book, How to Get Control of Your Time and Your Life. He recommends "poking holes" in a large task by using little bits of time instead of waiting for one large block of time. This technique can be extremely helpful when you want to get started on a project or to keep up momentum once you have begun.

The significance of the Swiss-cheese technique is that it advocates the value of any amount of time, no matter how small. Thirty minutes is valuable, fifteen minutes is valuable, and even in five minutes you can accomplish something. The fact that your report will require ten hours to prepare does not mean that you have to wait until you have a ten-hour block of time before you can start. You may find small bits of time by surprise. If a colleague cancels an appointment that was supposed to last for half an hour, you have just been given thirty minutes. If you finish your phone calls ten minutes before you have to leave the office, those ten minutes can be useful. Or you may employ the Swiss-cheese method as a way just to get started on a large task you're dreading. Decide to work on it for fifteen minutes, and no more. You'll poke a hole in it, and no matter how much or how little you accomplish, you won't still be avoiding it.

If you can get a little bit accomplished, you may feel good about it. Then the satisfaction you get from making progress can function as a reward. Believe it or not, you may be drawn to repeat the experience of working so that you'll feel good again. This is a real contrast to the way you probably use work to punish yourself. If you've been procrastinating, you may sentence yourself to solitary confinement for a whole weekend in order to catch up. But the mere thought of such confinement conjures up feelings of being chained to your desk while every one else is having fun. The prospect of a lonely arduous Sunday is not enticing, so you don't do it. Experience confirms what research has shown: Punishment is not a motivation. You're better off using a little carrot than a big stick.

Expect Interruptions and Disruptions

According to Murphy's Law, "Anything that can go wrong will go wrong." But many procrastinators don't believe that this rule of thumb will apply to them once they have finally made up their minds to get down to work. Why haven't you planned for the possibility that something could go wrong? Why assume that your effort is the only factor to consider? Things do go wrong at their usual rate. There are limits to what you can control. You can't get to the airport on time if there is a big traffic jam. If you acknowledge in advance the possibility of random disaster, you can plan your time to make allowances for disruptions. Then, when obstacles do inevitably occur, you are in a better position to take them in stride instead of feeling either frantic or futile.

Delegate

Delegating is a way to increase your efficiency and avoid putting things off. If you give some of your workload to someone else, then your burden is reduced and you are free to concentrate on the important tasks. The process of delegating involves: a) identifying tasks you alone don't have to do, b) finding the best person who could do it, c) making clear what needs to be done, and d) keeping track of how they're progressing. Delegating is a skill and not a failure. The real failure occurs when you're stubbornly holding on to every item in your life so that you stay bogged down. Another perfectionist pitfall is "I'm the only one who can do this right." Although there may be some things that you and only you can do, is that really true of everything on your list of unfinished chores? Even if someone else wouldn't do it in quite your way, there's greater advantage in having it done by a different approach than leaving it undone, waiting for your personal touch. Refusing help is a good way to put things off. If you try to "go it alone," you're increasing the pressure on yourself. Adding pressure, as we have been saying, is adding problems.

Something Has Got to Give

It is easy to get spread too thin. You say yes too many times. You take on too many interesting projects at once; you work more hours to make more money; you are the one everyone relies on for help. Before you know it, you're so busy that you don't have time to get everything done, and you're letting crucial things slide. Is being too busy the same thing as procrastinating? It can be if you use your busyness to avoid something more important. In adding on commitments, not only are you setting the stage for procrastination, but you're also giving yourself a ready excuse: "I'm not really procrastinating, I'm just too busy to get everything done on time."

Take a hard look at your commitments. Are you spread too thin? Is this a setup to procrastinate on something that matters? Aren't there things you really could give up? You'll lose something in the process, to be sure, but is it necessary for the sake of the greater goal?

Identify Your Prime Time

There is a natural rhythm to your day, and this rhythm is different for each of us. Think about when during the day you have the most mental energy; when you are most physically energetic; when you feel most sociable; and when you feel depleted. Do you get your second wind at five o'clock, eight o'clock, eleven o'clock, or not at all. Knowing your own rhythm will help you plan more realistically. Identifying your prime time means acknowledging that some of your time is less than prime. Nobody can work at top capacity all the time. You have to realize that you have human limits.

Take Leisure You Can Really Enjoy

It is ironic that procrastinators, by demanding so much of themselves, don't work, but they don't relax either. Even when you do things you love, the chances are you're not enjoying them 100 percent because you know you're using them to avoid something else. Or you may not even let yourself have these diversions because you feel unproductive and therefore undeserving. In either case you're not having real fun.

Pleasure is so important in life. Try to plan for it, and give it to yourself. Make time for things you really enjoy, and allow yourself to go ahead and do them without guilt or desperation. If you deprive yourself of true relaxation, you will run out of energy like a car runs out of gas. And you will steal leisure time by procrastinating.

(1382 words)

 Useful Phrases and Expressions

1. time-gobbling

2. I'll take a half-day off to do something.

3. I can knock off my annual report in an hour.

4. It's obvious that...

5. a whole lot longer

6. He is behind in his Russian literature class.

7. These estimates seem possible.

8. wishful thinking

9. Compare your predictions about how long things take with what actually happens.

10. everyday activities

11. Their predictions were way off when they actually take a measurement.

12. make a great suggestion for somebody

13. get control of your time and your life

14. use little bits of time

15. one large block of time

16. This technique can be extremely helpful when...

17. get started on a project

18. keep up momentum

19. The significance of the Swiss-cheese technique is that...

20. find something by surprise

21. employ the Swiss-cheese method as a way just to get started on

22. The satisfaction you get from making progress can function as a reward.

23. solitary confinement

24. be chained to your desk

25. The prospect of a lonely arduous Sunday is not enticing.

26. You're better off using a little carrot than a big stick.

27. Anything that can go wrong will go wrong.

28. make up their minds to get down to work

29. Things go wrong at their usual rate.

30. There are limits to what you can control.

31. random disaster

32. You are in a better position to do something.

33. Delegating is a way to increase your efficiency.

34. You are free to concentrate on the important.

35. make clear what needs to be done

36. Keep track of how they're progressing.

37. hold on to sht./sb.

38. You stay bogged down.

39. There's greater advantage in...

40. go it alone

41. your personal touch

42. It is easy to spread too thin.

43. take on too many interesting projects at once

44. You are the one everybody relies on for help.

45. get everything done

46. You're letting crucial things slide.

47. set the stage for

48. take a hard look at your commitments

49. You'll lose something in the process.

50. There is a natural rhythm to your day.

51. You have the most mental energy.

52. physically energetic

53. get your second wind

54. Nobody can work at top capacity all the time.

55. realize that you have human limits

56. It is ironic that...

57. Chances are that...

58. You feel unproductive, undeserving.

59. have real fun

60. Pleasure is so important in life.

 Exercises

Ⅰ.Comprehension Questions

1. What problem do many people have when they arrange their time?

2. Does this problem cause another problem? What is it?

3. Is there any way to counter this mismanagement of time?How?

4. What is "Swiss-cheese" method of time management?

5. Where does this method come from and who made this suggestion?

6. What is the significance of this method?

7. How does Swiss-cheese method help you not to put things off?

8. What is Murphy's Law?

9. What would you use this law to plan your time?

10. What should you do if you want to increase your efficiency and avoid putting things off?

11. What is another setup to procrastinate?

12. How can you avoid being spread yourself thin?

13. Why is it important to identify your prime time?

14. What do you have to know about yourself in terms of energy?

15. Why are procrastinators unproductive?

II .Essay Writing

Write an essay by putting together the answers to the questions in Exercise I, using such joining words as because, and, but and so on.

III .Questions for Discussion

1. Why do people put off things? Do you put off things? Are you going to correct this bad habit? Why?

2. What do you think of the suggestions in the passage? Are they realistic? Are they difficult to apply?

3. Do you think this passage has some practical value? Why do you think so?

IV .Translation

Put the following Chinese into English, using as many as possible the phrases and expressions you have learned.

1. 亞里士多德認為，人本質上是習慣的奴隸（creatures of habit）。如果我們要在其他人眼裡看起來很高尚，就得養成高尚的習慣。習慣是由行為不斷重複而形成的。在平時注意禮貌有助於我們養成好的習慣。我們眼中高尚、真誠、忠實的人與自私、刻薄、不好相處的人的區別，很大程度上和他們平時的小節和言行舉止有很大的關係。生活是由各種小事組成的，絕大多數人絕對不會去殺人或偷他人的汽車。通常我們認為一個人特別的好，絕不是因為他為消除貧困孜孜不倦地工作，而是平時他待人接物很有禮貌。

2. 對所有高階管理人員來說，時間是最寶貴的，他們每天最需要的是時間。很多高級管理人員常常抱怨沒有足夠的時間來處理事務，而經常無法完成計劃，他們發現由於太忙而把一些重要的事情耽誤了。為了趕計劃，他們經常加班加點，影響了健康，加班實際上給自己增加了壓力。在快速運轉的世界裡，一天中的每分鐘都有事要做，這是很自然的。但這並不意味著為了辦事你非得去犧牲健康，你的問題完全是由於時間安排不好。在這裡我給你提些建議：首先你要確定你的首要任務。通常事情分成四類：第一類，事情很重要，也很緊急；第二類，事情很重要，但不緊急；第三類，事情緊急，但不重要；第四類，事情既不重要又不緊急。要辦事先擬訂一個詳細的計劃，然後按計劃先辦重要又緊急的事情。你一定要把一切安排得很好，這樣才能一點一點地把工作做完，同時你不會感到面鋪得太大。另一件重要的事是把你的工作分擔一點給你的經理或部門主管，你一個人根本不可能把所有的事都辦了。如果你這樣做，你的工作效率就會大大地提高了。

國家圖書館出版品預行編目（CIP）資料

交際英語 / 朱正主編 . -- 第一版 . -- 臺北市：崧博出版：崧
燁文化發行 , 2019.02

　　面；　公分
POD 版
ISBN 978-957-735-678-9(平裝)

1. 英語 2. 口語 3. 會話

805.188　　　　　　　　　　　　　　108001901

書　　　名：交際英語

作　　　者：朱正 主編

發 行 人：黃振庭

出 版 者：崧博出版事業有限公司

發 行 者：崧燁文化事業有限公司

E - m a i l：sonbookservice@gmail.com

粉 絲 頁：▨　　　網 址：▨

地　　　址：台北市中正區重慶南路一段六十一號八樓 815 室

8F.-815, No.61, Sec. 1, Chongqing S. Rd., Zhongzheng

Dist., Taipei City 100, Taiwan (R.O.C.)

電　　　話：(02)2370-3310 傳　真：(02) 2370-3210

總 經 銷：紅螞蟻圖書有限公司

地　　　址：台北市內湖區舊宗路二段 121 巷 19 號

電　　　話:02-2795-3656 傳真 :02-2795-4100　　網址：▨

印　　　刷：京峯彩色印刷有限公司（京峰數位）

　　本書版權為旅遊教育出版社所有授權崧博出版事業股份有限公司獨家發行電子
書及繁體書繁體字版。若有其他相關權利及授權需求請與本公司聯繫。

定　　　價：400 元

發行日期：2019 年 02 月第一版

◎ 本書以 POD 印製發行